D1523895

THE
FINAL
ACT

BRUNO AMATO

BRUNO AMATO

First Edition 2021

Bruno dedicates this book to the love of his life, Stacey, who not only gave him heartfelt advice and a woman's perspective but, encouraged him to tell this story to the world.

Table of Contents

Chapter One

He was confident that tonight would be heaven, but by morning.... it could all go to hell.

"Don't look. It's a surprise."

Danny reached forward to rest his hands over Angie's eyes after he whispered the words near her ear. He guided his blonde goddess of a wife into their extravagant bedroom, an excited smile crossing his perfectly angled face that matched his shredded muscular body as he stopped her before she reached the bed.

"What are you up to?" Angie giggled as she came to a stop, her tone full of curiosity as she cocked her head a little to the side. An excited smile graced her lips, and they curled up at the sides.

"Just a little Valentine's Day surprise for my girl," Danny replied, leaning forward to peck her cheek adoringly. They had just gotten back from a nice dinner at their favorite restaurant, which overlooked the Pacific Ocean, and now Danny planned to end the night right with a surprise or two. He would do anything to keep a smile on her face because she made him the happiest man alive. He couldn't imagine his life without her.

"You know that I love surprises," Angie quipped as she shifted impatiently on the spot until Danny's hands slipped away from in front of her eyes, revealing a bed full of gifts. A large teddy bear sat in the center of the bed with a box of Godiva chocolates situated against one leg, a small jewelry box near the other, and a lacy, white pair of panties with red hearts adorning the material placed in the middle of them. She plucked up the panties and gave him a smirk.

Danny smiled innocently before accepting an excited hug from her, his hands wrapping around her waist to hold her tight. He was glad that she liked his arrangement since he had spent all day yesterday shopping around for the right gifts to give her. He felt like a teenager experiencing his first serious Valentine's Day with his girlfriend, making his heart threaten to beat right out of his chest.

"I've got a few Valentine's gifts for you as well," Angie purred, leaning forward to gently kiss him. Her arms wound around his neck, her fingers sifting up into his hair as he backed her up toward the bed. Once the back of her knees hit the edge of the mattress, she toppled down on top of it giggling and bringing Danny down with her. Danny shrugged innocently before accepting an excited hug from her, his hands wrapping around her waist to hold her tight. He was glad that she liked his arrangement since he had spent all week shopping around for the right gifts to give her. He felt like a teenager experiencing his first serious Valentine's Day with his girlfriend, making his heart threaten to beat right out of his chest, yet Angie was his wife and he was thrilled he still felt like this about her. It was an amazing evening for both of them. Danny would surely sleep well tonight....

Stark sunlight poured through the kitchen window of Danny's childhood home, which was an apartment, but it was home, nonetheless. His home was wherever his mother and younger brother were. Danny stood from the dining table where he and his younger brother were sitting to walk into the kitchen behind his mother as she stirred pasta around in a pot on the stove, soft humming drifting from her. Danny wrapped his small fingers around the handle of the refrigerator before yanking hard, the door nearly knocking his seven-year-old self onto the hard tile floor, but he steadied himself before searching for the carton of milk.

"Danny, I told you to watch your brother. Please go find him," his mother sighed softly, the worried wrinkles in her forehead making her look older than her thirty years.

Danny turned around with a confused look on his face, having just been sitting at the table with his younger brother. To his surprise, his brother wasn't at the table anymore. He shut the refrigerator door before heading out of the front door and over to the stairwell in their apartment building. He saw his little brother at the bottom of the stairs on his way out of the building.

"Hey! Where are you going!" Danny cried out to him, but his brother ignored him. Danny tore down the staircase and out the door into the Los Angeles sun, the heat making him wince. Strangely, the street was eerily quiet today instead of being bustling and busy like usual. He glanced to his left to catch a glimpse of his younger brother about to enter a bar a few doors down. Danny took off after him, trying to catch him before he went inside, but he wasn't fast enough.

Danny paused outside of the bar, his head tilting up to look at the red and black flashing neon sign that hung above the door. He could hear the heavy thumping of rockabilly music playing from inside of the small building, and his nerves grew worse. Despite them, he struggled to pull the heavy wooden door open so that he could step inside. A gust of smoke sent him coughing, his nose wrinkling at the smell of cigarettes as he stepped through into the pub.

The people crowding the inside were tattooed and aggressive, spewing lewd words and sharp curses. They looked unsavory and suspicious. A few of the patrons eyed Danny as he cautiously crept through the bar, prompting them to laugh among themselves. Danny couldn't see his brother anywhere, but he needed to keep looking so that Danny could get him out of this strange place. He walked past a few tables near the bar area until a middle-aged female stripper stepped in front of him to block his way and view. She was clad in only a flimsy bikini with a cocktail in one hand a few crumbled dollar bills in the other.

"You're a little young to be in here," the stripper winked at him, batting her big glue-on eyelashes.

"I'm looking for my brother," Danny awkwardly stated, his eyes shifting to the side to spot a soldier in army fatigues, who was sitting with his back to Danny. Empty shot glasses covered the table around him as smoke drifted from the end of the cigarette that he was holding. Danny lifted his hand to wave at the soldier, trying to get his attention.

"Excuse me, sir," Danny called out.

An old, wasted couple that sat next to the soldier glanced over at Danny, their eyes glassy and their smiles loose as they waved at him drunkenly. The old man then turned to the soldier, patting his arm to capture his attention and then direct it toward Danny.

The soldier slowly turned around.

Danny tilted his head up to look at the soldier, his eyes widening in shock when he saw that the soldier's face was completely bloodied. The front of the soldier's shirt was ripped open with a gash in his chest as well. A gasp of horror broke from Danny, and he fell backward, shuffling on the floor as the soldier approached him. Danny hurriedly pushed himself to his feet, scrambling to get away from the horrifying soldier and out of that place as fast as he could.

When Danny got halfway to the exit of the bar, he realized that he couldn't run any faster. His eyes shot down to see that his feet were sunk down in two feet of heavy mud. Panicked breaths left him as he tried to lift his feet out of the mud, but every effort was futile. He pitched a look behind him to see the soldier's hand reaching out and mouthing the words "help me," from his bloodied mouth.

With a gasp, Danny opened his eyes, the darkness of his bedroom greeting him as he panted heavily, his body now drenched with sweat. He lifted his hand to press over his eyes, trying to wipe the remnants of the nightmare away, but they always stayed with him no matter what. They haunted him like ghosts that could never be put to rest. He eventually lowered his shaky hand to pitch a look over to the side at Angie sleeping quietly next to him, her bare back facing him. At least he hadn't woken her.

Trying to ground himself, Danny turned his stare to the large chandelier above him. The crystals absorbed and reflected the soft rays of early morning sunlight that reached in through the bedroom window, casting rainbow prisms along the ceiling and walls. The sight was much brighter than the scenes of his nightmares, from which he wished he could one day escape.

Chapter Two

It was a beautiful day in Hollywood, California, the bright sun blazing from an electric blue sky barely marred by a few dense yet fluffy white clouds. Yet today was like most days in this city of angels.

The mere mention of Hollywood conjured up images of studio lots, movie premieres, and stars from all eras: Chaplin, Monroe, Bogart, Poitier, DiCaprio, Zellweger... The list went on.

A town like no other, where so many had travelled over the years filled with dreams of 'making it,' though the vast majority never did. Hollywood chewed 'em up and spit 'em out.

And it wasn't that they weren't talented. Some, almost all, just never got that 'big break.'

Danny Vitello was one of the lucky ones. He got his break as a kid. Sure, he didn't have to travel far, he grew up in LA, but being an actor never crossed his mind.

Some of the teenage kids he went to school with had different ideas, or their parents did. One day, Danny tagged along with a buddy of his who had an audition. Well, the casting people loved what they saw, but Danny ended up getting that commercial, not his friend.

It was pretty obvious from the start; Danny had that special something. You couldn't really put a finger on it, but you liked it. Before long, Danny had an agent, Max Steinberg, who was happy to take 10% of everything Danny earned. And Danny was earning. He started out playing the hunky boyfriend on a couple Lifetime movies and graduated to series regular on a hit sitcom that aired on television for three seasons. He became a heartthrob to millions of young fans across the country. He had the smile, the green eyes, luscious dark hair, and a set of abs the producers always made sure were exposed at some point during the show. Next thing you know, Danny was doing movies and attending red carpet premieres. But unlike any other movie star, at least since Jimmy Stewart, Danny volunteered to join the service, the US Army to be exact. He went off to war in the Middle East and saw things people shouldn't see. He made it back alive, but he still sees those things, almost every night. And then morning comes.

This morning was like so many others, marked by the enthusiasm with which people attack the day with gusto from behind the cover of cars, honking in persistence to be let through the inevitable traffic jam at this time on the 101 Freeway.

One of them, in a sleek Mercedes convertible, sipping a black Starbucks coffee from his right hand and gripping his steering wheel in another, sent out wordless cusses to the hulking truck ahead of him that couldn't figure out which lane to stay in. His only beam of happiness came from the billboard by the right side of the freeway.

It had a picture of a man in his prime, mid-thirties, soulful eyes, a mysterious smile and a calm arrogance that invited the audience to dare not applaud his performance in HYDE.

That was Danny up on that billboard for all those on the road to see. Hyde was his latest and probably biggest movie to date, and according to that sign, he was the best thing on screen in years.

Danny's fingers drummed against the top of his steering wheel as he waited in the line of cars to enter the gates of Paramount Studios. The sun was scorching the City of Angels, prompting him to shift his dark Ray-Bans up more on the bridge of his nose to block out the sunlight that glinted off of the hood of his shiny car. He fluffed out the front of his V-neck T-shirt, trying to let the air conditioning under his clothes to cool himself down. As he waited, he reached past his Starbucks cup in the middle console to grab a movie script in his passenger seat that was flipped to a page highlighted in yellow. He glanced over a few lines before looking up into his rearview mirror.

"YOU said you'd have the money by now!" he bellowed before looking down at the script, shaking his head, and then looking back up at the mirror again.

"You said you'd have MY money by now!" he tried again, but he groaned in disgust. He threw the script back down on the passenger seat.

"Man, that is some garbage," Danny muttered to himself before his cell phone started to ring. He hit the speaker button on his car dashboard to channel the call through.

"You got Danny."

"Danny, sorry for the late notice. Richie can't make it in. We're gonna shut down production for the day," the assistant director's voice came on over the car's speaker.

Danny withheld a disappointed sigh as he settled back in his seat.

"Is he alright?" he asked.

"He's out near those fires in Malibu. A lot of the roads are blocked. Hope you didn't drive in yet," the assistant director replied sheepishly.

Danny glanced up at the main entrance to Paramount Studios before shaking his head, not believing his bad luck today. It hadn't started great, and it wasn't getting any better.

"Don't worry about it. See ya tomorrow," Danny told him casually before hanging up. He wasted all of this time fighting traffic to get all of the way there just to have to go back. He drove near the studio guard shack, tossing his hand out of the window to signal to the gate guard that he was doing a U-turn. He whipped around and then tore away, smoke puffing away from his tires.

Danny would make lemonade out of the huge sack of lemons life had just handed him by going to visit his wife on set.

Angie was shooting over in Glendale. With traffic at this hour, it would only take him about eighty-five thousand hours to get to her, and it would be worth it. 'Love' seemed like such a meager word compared to how he felt about Angie. Sharing a bed, a house, and all of his off hours with her never seemed to be enough. Like the wildfire raging out in Malibu, Danny's love for Angie was hot, expansive, and perhaps unstoppable.

Danny cruised Melrose Ave. before parking in front of *Tilly's Flower Shop*. He pulled to a stop in front of an array of silky red roses, blushing hibiscus, angelic white daisies, and tear drop light irises. He could already smell their fresh fragrances.

The owner, a plump woman with iron grey hair and sharp black eyes, strolled out to see who was blocking her business.

Her weathered face broke into smiles when she spotted Danny behind the wheel, unhindered by the black shades blocking his eyes.

"Danny...whatchu doin' in the car? Come in, I'll make some espresso," she invited, beaming.

Danny tossed her his first genuine smile that morning, "Nah Tilly, another time," he said and ducked lower in his car. He'd spotted a pap guy pointing a camera lens at him.

Tilly noticed too and straightened, the beatific smile never leaving her face. "Her favorites?" she asked.

Danny nodded, "The best of the bunch."

"You know I only carry the best," Tilly said as she was selecting long stemmed irises and a mix of sunflowers. After she was done, she tied them in a neat efficient bow and handed them to Danny. "A burst of colors for a beautiful lady." She'd never really understood why Angie liked such common flowers and mixed so oddly, too.

She gave a quick glance at the paparazzi guy who was inching closer and said, "I'll just put it on your tab, Danny."

Danny gave her a grateful smile and screeched out of the shop into the hectic morning traffic.

By the time he got to Angie's movie lot, Danny had completely gotten over the scheduling catastrophe. There were people in the industry who would have killed for an unexpected day off. Danny clutched the bouquet of colorful flowers as he strode past various dressing room trailers, smiling back at extras and crew members that scurried around and nodded to him. He was incredibly proud of Angie's success and notable talent, and he wanted to be as supportive of her as she was toward him. They were a team, a power couple in their own right. He couldn't begin to describe how lucky he felt to have her all to himself.

A female production assistant in her twenties popped up in front of him, holding a clipboard and a walkie-talkie. She was wide-eyed and glowing, her brown hair pulled tight in a high ponytail to keep it out of her way.

"Hey, Mr. Vitello! How's it going?" she chirped, giving him a friendly smile.

"Pretty good. I was hoping to surprise her," Danny replied as he held up the flowers he was holding.

The production assistant beamed even brighter at his words and placed her hand over her heart.

"Oh, she'll love those! Her trailer's the big one on the end," she told him, pointing to a bunch of trailers parked next to each other not too far down the lot.

"Thanks," Danny answered gratefully, watching her dart off to attend to something else. He straightened up and headed to the trailer with "Angie Swan" on the door, an excited smile crossing his face as he knocked and waited for her to open the door. However, there was no answer. He reached forward to try the door handle, but it was locked. He knocked one more time before calling for her.

"Angie?!"

Suddenly, the door flew open. Angie popped her head out to look at Danny, a look of shock rippling across her face before she slapped a plastic smile on top of it to cover it up.

"Oh my gosh, Danny! Hi! What are you doing here? I thought you were filming," she rambled through her words, looking tense as she blocked the doorway to her trailer.

"Our director couldn't make it in, so we postponed until tomorrow. Figured I'd come see my superstar wife in action," Danny explained with a little smile, finding it amusing how surprised and flustered she was to see him. He had really caught her off guard, but she did love surprises.

Angie shifted on the spot awkwardly, her lips parting, but no words left her.

"Wow … what a nice surprise. Get in here! I-I was just running lines with Brett," Angie explained, her voice coming out a bit weak as she stepped aside to let Danny enter the trailer.

Danny stepped inside, glancing around at the well-furnished interior. He noticed Brett Malone, Angie's costar, sitting on a small couch with a script in his hands. He was also in his thirties with devilishly good looks, a known heartthrob in the movie scene. Danny gave him an inquisitive look as Brett shifted awkwardly on the couch, seeming a bit squirrely.

"Danny! Wow! Big fan. How's it going?" Brett asked, chuckling in a nervous manner. He stood from the couch, extending his hand out to Danny for a handshake.

Angie glanced over and noticed the flowers that Danny still had in his hand as he curiously glanced between her and Brett.

"Look at those beautiful flowers! Here, let me put them in something," Angie voiced, reaching forward to take the flowers from Danny. She looked down and noticed her pair of lacy, white panties with red hearts on them sticking out of Brett's back pocket.

Brett shook Danny's hand, a stiff smile on his face.

"Your wife is killing it out there. Glad I'm getting the chance to work with her," Brett told him.

Angie stole an anxious glance at Brett over Danny's shoulder, realizing that Brett had no clue about the panties sticking out of his pocket. She filled a big glass of water and placed the flowers in it before carrying the glass over closer by Danny.

"Danny, we finally shot the getaway scene today. The DP was crammed in the car with us, doing close ups," Angie started to explain.

"It was definitely tight inside there," Brett broke in to add.

Angie drew in a nervous breath before turning and accidentally dropping the flowers, the glass shattering on the wooden floor of the trailer.

"Damn it! I'm so clumsy!" she cursed, a flush of anxiety rushing through her as she stood over the pieces of glass and flowers.

"Let me help," Brett volunteered as he grabbed a few paper towels before bending down near the mess.

Danny moved forward to help pick up the glass, carefully grabbing the bigger shards off of the floor. His eyes shifted over as Brett stood up to throw away the wet paper towels, his focus soon zeroing in on the familiar pair of panties sticking out of Brett's pocket. Wordlessly, he gaped up at Angie, their eyes clashing intensely.

"Danny, don't!" Angie exclaimed, already seeing the fire growing in Danny's eyes.

Danny did. He jumped to his feet, his vision a red haze as he lunged at Brett, slamming the other man down to the ground. He struck down at Brett, knocking his fist against Brett's face over and over until things went black.

When he came to, Danny glanced around to see the trailer's interior in shambles. Glass and blood littered the wooden flooring. Angie held Brett's bloodied face in her hands as he laid on the floor, limp and moaning.

Danny found himself running out of the trailer, getting to his car as fast as he could without looking back. He was afraid to stay because he might finish what he started, and anger made his body tremble all the way to his fingertips.

Once he gunned his car to life, Danny peeled out of the trailer lot, a cloud of dirt kicking up from his tires as they spun rapidly. He tore down the coastal highway, the Pacific Ocean to his right, his vision blurred by the vivid thoughts of what just occurred.

Danny couldn't believe that Angie had done such a thing to him, ripping his heart out and stomping on it repeatedly without a care in the world. He had given her those panties, given her his heart. He was sickened, his mind dipping into a dark red, cloudy haze that wouldn't lift. He was stuck in internal chaos.

Ahead of his car was a Volkswagen Bus with a surfboard rack that had two boards on top. It drove slowly, prompting Danny to whip around it to fly past it. He ignored the honking, not caring about how fast and wild he was driving. He just had to get as far away from Angie as possible. Maybe the pain would lessen the farther that he got from her.

Up ahead on the shoulder of the road, Danny's eyes focused in on two barricades with warning signs reading "DANGEROUS CLIFFS AHEAD," but that didn't deter him at all. In fact, it encouraged him to slam his foot down on the gas even more, his hand guiding the steering wheel in the direction of the barricades. He hurtled toward them, his car smashing through the wooden posts and flying toward the treacherous cliffs below. Danny didn't see what happened next, the dark red coloring fading into black once again.

The first thing Danny noticed when he came back around was the pressure of a deployed airbag and shattered glass cutting into his face. He blinked his eyes open, a deep soreness overtaking his body. He lifted his

14

head slowly, his eyes looking into the cracked rearview mirror to see a gash above his eye and a trail of blood running from his nose. He dropped his eyes a little to see that his windshield was shattered, and that smoke poured from the hood of his car, which was wedged into a big boulder. It was a miracle that he was alive. Just then, a hand touched his shoulder, making him flinch.

"Hey, pal. Are you okay?" a husky trucker asked as he leaned in towards Danny.

Danny tenderly turned his head to the side to gaze at the trucker, his body tense and aching.

"Lucky for you, that big ass rock got in your way. It's a long way down. A few more feet to the right, you'd have been a goner," the trucker sighed, nodding to the open space that Danny's car could've fallen through.

Danny merely groaned, unable to find the strength to even speak. Pain echoed throughout every inch of his body, making him wince and shut his eyes, wishing that the ache would go away.

The only thing good about the physical ache was that it took his focus away from the emotional pain that he had let consume him before he drove his car toward the cliffs.

"Try not to move. I called 911 and … hey, ain't you the guy from that movie with …" the trucker's voice trailed off into a muted muffle that Danny couldn't hear anymore.

Danny slumped back down against the airbag, only able to hear the slow, deep chop of the crashing waves nearby. He fell into the noise, letting it fill his head and wash over the red that took over him.

Chapter Three

Two years later

Every artist was well aware of World Endeavors Talent Agency and its powerful grip on the entertainment world. At its head was Max Steinberg, the ultimate force and voice in Hollywood, who had artists nearly groveling at his feet just to get him to give them a look their way. He was all powerful, and everyone knew it.

Max rapidly typed away at his keyboard in his office, glass panels acting as his walls so that he could look out at everyone who worked for him. He set an example of the work ethic that he expected from the rest of the people in the company. If they didn't match up with him, World Endeavors would be a failure, a laughingstock, and that would not pass with him. He jammed his forefinger against the exclamation mark key before settling back in his swivel chair to read his message to one of the hundreds of clients that he worked with.

You NEED to go to that interview! No excuses!

Feeling like he got his point across, Max sent the email and sighed, drifting his hand through the greying strands of his hair. At sixty-five, he should've been working out his retirement plan, whether he wanted to buy a condo in West Palm Beach or leave the country entirely to die with a drink in his hand and a tan on his skin. However, Hollywood was so beautifully addictive, drawing him back in to the endless cycle of writing up contracts for large sums of money and badgering studios and networks for better deals.

It was hard to break away from something that was working out so well for him. His cut of the deals was sufficient, and he worked with mostly A-list actors and performers who were the real deal. He didn't have enough life left to waste his time on people who didn't have a chance making it to the studio or the stage. However, even the popular clients could be a pain, like he was trying to round up kids hopped up on sugar. They were destructive to their own careers and acted like they were blameless. He had to come up behind them and clean up the mess.

As tiring as the work was, Max wouldn't choose to do anything else. He smoothed down the charcoal gray material of his Armani suit before sitting back up closer to his desk. He sent off another email to a whining client, who decided to have a mental breakdown on his Twitter and lose half of his fanbase in one night. His secretary's voice sounded over the intercom of his desk phone.

"Mr. Steinburg, Danny Vitello is on line two," she announced clearly.

Max let the first call go to voicemail as he sighed.

"He's not calling from jail, right?" Max asked as he pinched the bridge of his nose.

"Well ... I don't think so," his secretary said, but her voice harbored doubt.

"Great," Max grunted before drawing in a deep breath and accepting the call, tapping the button to take it.

"Danny! Long time!" Max feigned cheer as his voice bellowed through the speaker.

"Max, thank you for taking my call," Danny's voice sounded quieter through the speaker, almost hesitant.

Max threaded his fingers together and placed them in his lap to keep them from tapping on the surface of his desk.

"Anything for you, Danny Boy. What can I do for you?" Max asked, nearly wincing as he waited for the answer.

Danny was silent for a few seconds, awkward tension filling the quietness until he finally spoke in a reluctant voice.

"Well … I was just … um …" Danny stumbled over his words, unable to say what needed to be said.

"I didn't quite catch that, Danny. What was that?" Max prompted him to actually speak a coherent sentence this time, trying to keep any agitation from sounding in his tone.

"I … I was hoping that you'd maybe … rep me again," Danny finally got the words out.

Max kept a sigh from breaking from him, his grip on his fingers tightening a degree as he shook his head a little.

"You know that I'm still working with Brett. Brett Malone," Max reminded Danny, not liking how pained Danny still sounded. It just wasn't good for business.

"Yeah, I figured … I mean …" Danny stammered before trailing off, unable to find any other words to say about that.

"Six weeks, Danny. One of my biggest client's! His mouth was wired shut for SIX weeks," Max gritted out. That had been an unexpected debacle that he had to deal with. It was a complete nightmare, and he didn't want to face the risk of another incident like that happening all over again.

"Yeah, well, he was screwing my wife! My WIFE! Did you forget that little detail?" Danny immediately snapped, anger seething in his words. The wound was obviously still open.

Max shook his head, his jaw clenching a degree. That temper was the reason for that whole mess happening in the first place. He couldn't trust Danny to keep it under control. He kept quiet as he rested his hand on his computer mouse and shifted it to click on the file labeled "headshots."

"We go back a long way, Max. We were like family, remember?" Danny said, his voice calming and cooling down.

Max's eyes shifted over to a shot of a gorgeous blonde before he nearly snorted at Danny's comment.

"Yeah, want to know what I remember? You, on *Hollywood Tonight*, threatening to break your interviewer's face and tearing up their studio," Max said pointedly.

"But …" Danny started to explain.

"That was on live television, Danny," Max cut in abruptly, his words coming out sharp.

"Come on, Max. I was going through a rough time, and you knew that," Danny groaned out, his voice bordering on pleading.

"You were supposed to win back the public's love and support by explaining yourself! Whatever, forget that. You were the lead in a franchise movie! A franchise movie, not some indie flick. We worked years to get to that level, and you quit without any notice! Just like that, after all those fucking years!" Max snapped, plainly ranting at this point. It had been disaster after disaster, and just thinking about it made his blood pressure rise.

"I know … I know. I messed up. I messed everything up, but … please, Max," Danny said, the last words coming out so faint that Max could hardly hear them.

However, the suppressed pride and the evident pain in Danny's voice made Max pause for a few moments. He breathed in slowly as he rubbed at his stubbled chin, his eyes hazing over as he thought hard. He had managed Danny Vitello since the beginning of his career. Danny had talent, there was no doubt about that, but that temper would have to be dealt with.

"I'll think about it," Max told him, only able to offer that for now. He would have to do more thinking on it, if Danny was worth the possible trouble and risk he could cause. Max wanted to retire in peace, not go down in flames.

"Thanks, man," Danny replied, relief sounding in his voice.

Max heard a click soon after as the line went dead.

Miles away from Max's glass-walled office, in a rundown apartment in the sleazier section of East Hollywood, Danny stared down at the dark, cracked screen of his phone with a similarly broken expression. His life had turned upside down, shaking up his reality and taking away every good thing about his life. He had lost his mansion in the Hollywood Hills, his exotic cars, his career, and his money, which was sucked up by various lawsuits for damages to Brett's face, breaking his movie contracts, the IRS, and the divorce.

His eyes trailed along the marked-up walls of his dimly lit one-bedroom apartment as he considered hurling his broken phone against the wall. However, he pushed those thoughts away, reminding himself of the few bills left in his wallet. He dropped his head with a sigh before collapsing on the old brown couch that he was sure his landlord had pulled out of a dumpster. The carpeting of the apartment was a dark shade of brown with strange stains scattered throughout the material. The kitchen was attached to the living room and had a sink that always leaked no matter how many times maintenance had claimed to fix it. He just let it drip at this point.

His bedroom had a small twin bed and a tiny TV set that rested on a large cardboard box. He spent most of his time laying around watching that television numbly and only leaving to grab some food, maybe a couple beers somewhere or even a movie, but always disguised as best he could with a cap and dark shades. Most days, it was just too hard to leave the apartment. He felt like every time he left, there was potential for him to be ruined all over again.

However, he hoped that working with Max again would turn things around. He could only let himself be miserable for so long. Two years was enough. He reached forward to place his phone on the wooden coffee table in front of the couch, his eyes drifting over to a picture that was face down on its surface. Tentatively, he reached out to grab the picture and look at it, his expression softening at the sight of the wedding photo. Angie had been the happiest bride that day. His fingertips drifted across her beaming face, memories flooding back from that day and the ones that followed. As he started recalling the whole trailer incident, he shook his head and placed the picture back down on the coffee table.

Danny felt that signature flow of heat rushing through him, grating on his nerves. It was so hard not to just explode when he thought of that day and how it had led to the downfall of his life. It all seemed like a nightmare.

Danny made his way to the fridge, which ran noisily, like it was about to fall apart. He spotted his orange tabby cat, Buddy, following him to the kitchen. Buddy had kept him somewhat sane since Danny had gotten him. He was a good beacon of comfort and distraction. Deciding to also get something to eat to also further distract himself, Danny took out three cans of beer and a piece of steak from the fridge.

After cracking open one can and downing half of it in one go, he set the can down before digging through his kitchen cabinets for a frying pan. He set it on the stove and set the gas to medium heat before throwing the steak on there with a few seasonings.

"Eating good tonight, Buddy," Danny smiled, leaning down to scratch the cat between his ears before grabbing his cans of beer and heading back to the couch as the steak started to heat up and sizzle in the pan. He downed the first can of beer, the second and third soon following. His head began to feel heavy as he rested it against the back of the couch.

"Should probably check the steak," Danny mumbled slowly, his eyelids fluttering a few times. He thought that he felt himself stand from the couch, but his body felt numb as he slipped into darkness.

"Get down! Get down! Sniper on the roof!"

Danny's body wasn't numb anymore. He was running, his boots kicking their way through the sandy area fifteen miles outside of Baghdad. The heat around him was dry and still, settling on his body like an extra layer of skin. Bullets whistled past his head as pained screams sounded from all around him, prompting him to dive down toward the ground to escape the shots ringing out.

Danny grunted as he hit the floor of his living room, his shoulder crashing into the coffee table. He snapped out of the memory, but he almost felt like he was still there since smoke filled the room and the fire alarm kept screaming at him. He hurriedly pushed himself to his feet, his knees nearly buckling as his body trembled. He stumbled to the kitchen to see the black and charred remains of his steak, smoke billowing from the pan. He quickly tossed the pan into the sink and ran the water before grabbing a dishtowel and waving it in front of the sensor, desperate to silence it.

"Turn off, damnit!" Danny growled as the alarm refused to stop shrieking. He pressed the only button that he saw on its white surface, but nothing worked. Anger struck him like lightning, prompting him to press the button again, but he used his whole fist instead. The cheap plastic immediately cracked before falling to the floor in multiple pieces, silence finally falling on the apartment.

A sigh of relief left Danny as he gazed around his smoke-filled apartment, his eyes falling on Buddy, who was cowering beneath the coffee table with his tail puffed, on alert for any other sign of danger. Danny crouched near the coffee table, reaching under it to gently drift his hand along Buddy's back.

"I'm sorry, Buddy. It's okay," he said before hearing a knock on the door. Something about that sound made dread flood through him. He wished that whoever was there would just leave.

After hearing another series of heavy knocks, Danny groaned and stood up to head to the door, pulling it open to reveal none other than the landlord, Mr. Baccala, an old, frail Italian man with numerous wrinkles spanning his olive-toned skin. There were only a few wisps of white hair left on the man's head. Despite his harmlessly older look, he had the power to evict Danny.

"Mr. Baccala, how are you?" Danny welcomed in a fake, cheery tone. He forced a plastic smile onto his face, knowing that his hair was sticking up and that his eyes were bloodshot and teary from all of the smoke.

"What happen?" Mr. Baccala asked in an Italian accent as he looked Danny up and down with a confused look. He leaned to the side to try to peer into Danny's wrecked and smoky apartment.

Danny leaned his own body to block Mr. Baccala's view, feeling Buddy ram his head against the back of his calf. Gently, he nudged Buddy back a bit.

"Nothing, just the smoke alarm went off. It's taken care of," Danny replied with a dismissive wave of his hand. He didn't want Mr. Baccala to think that he was stirring up any sort of trouble. The last thing that he needed right now was to be kicked out of his apartment.

"I know. I heard it. What was all the yelling and banging?" Mr Baccala asked pointedly, crossing his thin arms over his bony chest.

Danny parted his lips to reply, but no answer came out. He couldn't think up a good one beyond that he thought that he was in Afghanistan. He would get a weird look for that one and probably an eviction notice.

"That thing is just really loud, and I was cooking. I dropped a pan," Danny tried to explain, hoping that was a good enough excuse.

Mr. Baccala nodded, shifting on the spot a little in a manner that made Danny realize he already knew what his landlord was about to say.

"My wife … she say your rent check bounce again. We like you … but we can't have you live here no more," Mr. Baccala said with a shake of his head.

Danny felt his heart drop into his stomach at the words, despair flooding through him.

"Just give me until the end of the month. I'll have the money for sure," he told Mr. Baccala, begging him with his eyes. He couldn't get kicked out because he didn't know where to go. He had no one. His eyes caught on to the silver Rolex on his wrist. His fingers trembled anxiously as he unclasped it and held it out to Mr. Baccala.

"Here, take it. It's a good one. I'll have your money by the end of the month. I promise you," Danny tried to negotiate, hoping that Mr. Baccala would just give him a chance. That was all that he needed.

Mr. Baccala shook his head at first, but his eyes widened a little at the nice look of the watch. He held up his own wrist that had a much less expensive watch on it.

"What am I going to do with another watch?"

Danny swallowed hard, trying to force down the lump in his throat as he waited for Mr. Baccala's next words.

"Fine. I give you until end of month," Mr. Baccala conceded as he uncrossed his arms.

A grateful look crossed Danny's face.

"Thank you, Mr. Baccala," he told the older man appreciatively.

The old man nodded and shuffled back down the dimly lit hallway.

Danny shut the door and leaned his forehead against it, his chest aching from the heavy beating of his heart.

Chapter Four

Brett Malone shifted in the director's chair, which was placed on the golden sand of this vast beach. The blue ocean rolled and crashed in front of him, the bright sun's reflection gleaming on its surface.

Brett leaned back in his seat, letting the breeze ruffle his Hawaiian shirt, which was paired with white shorts. His feet were bare and buried in the warm sand. He was shooting in Hawaii, but it was no vacation. He was hounded by someone at every turn, including the make-up artist, who was trying to edge toward him again to finish. Luckily, his phone ringing saved him.

"What's up, Max?" Brett sighed into the phone, knowing that this had to be important since Max was calling in the middle of a major shoot. If it wasn't, that would only add to the list of things that were annoying him today. He didn't want to be talking to anybody that he didn't have to.

"So, something crazy happened today. Danny called," Max started to explain as he stared through one of the glass walls of his office, mindlessly watching some of the other employees working away at their desks. He noticed that the ones closest to his office worked harder than the rest.

"He wants me to represent him again," Max finished, delivering the kicker.

Brett immediately sat up in his chair, his eyes widening out of surprise.

"Danny ... Vitello?" Brett asked for clarification to make sure that he heard right, because it sounded like Max was talking about the Danny that nearly split his face in two and almost ruined his career.

"Yeah." Max tensed, preparing for the backlash. He couldn't exactly blame Brett for that, but this was still business. Everyone was happier when personal matters were kept out of it. However, most stars didn't get that memo and showed all of their dirty laundry to everyone who would look. It was messy and troublesome.

"Well, I hope you told him to go fuck himself, because if you represent him, you don't represent me, comprendo?" Brett snapped. He figured this was just a ploy for Danny to get close enough to come back after Angie.

Max exhaled, rolling his eyes up toward the ceiling.

"Of course I told him that. I mean, not in those exact words, but ..." Max started to reply as he rubbed at his temple with his fingers. He was already starting to get a headache from this conversation. Then, he heard a beep on Brett's end.

"Good, look, I have to take this call," Brett cut Max off as he glanced at his phone to see who was calling him now. A smirk immediately crossed his lips when he realized who it was.

"It's Angie. Bye," Brett added before accepting Angie's call and ending the one with Max, not caring to hear another word on that end. As long as Max did his job and didn't piss him off by representing Danny, things would be just fine. He didn't need anyone crossing him.

"Hey, doll," Brett smiled into the phone as he relaxed back into his chair, his eyebrows lifting out of intrigue.

Angie perched on the edge of the large, shimmering pool, her red-painted toes kicking slowly through the water. A one-piece suit gripped the slim curve of her figure, while the dark Dolce and Gabbana sunglasses shielded her blue eyes from the beaming sun from up above. She held the latest edition of *Tinseltown Magazine* in her lap, gazing down at the cover photo of her and Brett on the front. They had been out on a date and leaving the restaurant when the photo had been taken without them knowing. The caption of *Hollywood's Hottest* gave her a slightly unsettling feeling that she could not shake.

"What are you up to?" Angie asked with a light smile before switching the magazine out for a glass of champagne.

"Just working and missing you, babe," Brett replied, his tone sounding flirtatious.

Angie bit her lip briefly, crossing her legs to capture the warmth that seeped between them.

"You're still coming home this weekend, right?" Angie asked him.

"Of course, baby. I can't wait to see your gorgeous self," Brett told her, smirking to himself as he spoke to her, looking forward to another weekend spent in the bedroom. He could use some relief from all the work that he had been doing lately on set. A shadow fell across his body, prompting him to look up to see Claudia, one of the set assistants, who gestured behind her urgently before walking away. Brett's eyes trailed her, admiring the curves of her hips as she walked.

"Babe, I gotta go. We're about to shoot, so I'll talk to you later. Miss you," Brett reeled off the words quickly as he hurriedly hopped off the chair.

"Miss you, too," Angie said softly, right as she heard the call disconnect mid-sentence. She set her cell phone down on the magazine before taking a deep sip of her champagne, enjoying its slight burn. Despite just talking to him, her thoughts weren't on Brett. They were on a different time, on another set, on another man, one who would ensure that she was happy and perfectly fine before hanging up the phone on her. She missed that man.

Danny found himself sitting on his couch, his eyes staring up at the blank ceiling. His wallet was empty. His heart was empty. There wasn't much left to him or his life, and he knew that.

He couldn't believe how far he had fallen over the past year, having struck bottom with no ability to launch back. He couldn't help but wonder if he would be stuck here forever. At one time, acting roles were offered to him, and he rarely ever had to audition. The remembrance of that prompted his head to snap up, as he grabbed his keys and headed over to Johnny's Hollywood Grill.

The neighborhood sports bar wasn't anything special, but it was cozy, and the beer was cheap, which meant that he could keep it flowing. That was all that mattered. As he walked into the familiar space, his eyes glancing over the photos of beloved sports players on the walls, he drew in a deep breath, letting himself settle into the space. He slid himself onto one of the tall stools by the bar, not bothering to acknowledge the few other patrons around. He just wanted to be alone with his beer.

"I'll take a Coors," he said to the bartender as she approached the counter.

She was in her mid-twenties, her curvy body threatening to show through the skimpy material of her white, sleeveless blouse which accentuated her tattoo-sleeved right arm. Bright pink hair fell against her exposed shoulders, matching the shimmering pink lipstick.

Danny didn't miss the flirty smiles that she passed his way, but he couldn't find an ounce of care for them. He merely took the glass of chilled beer that she placed in front of him and directed his eyes to the small television above the counter that was behind her head. He wasn't aiming to be rude, but it was hard to even interact with people nowadays.

Just as LeBron was about to score, the door of the bar burst open, three men stumbling through it at an obnoxiously loud volume. One of the men tapped the biggest one on the right.

"Yo! Big Tony! Check out the fox behind the counter," he chuckled crudely, his eyebrows lifting out of interest.

Big Tony openly gawked at the bartender, a whistle leaving his lips as he slapped the third man on the back, who was the smallest of the group with a shaved head. The style was probably done in his attempt to look tougher, but it just made him look scrawnier.

"Lonnie! Damn! … she looks like your old lady!" Big Tony howled, sending all three of them cracking up loudly.

Danny gritted his teeth a little in annoyance, his eyes rolling as he focused on the television. To his dismay, the three men sat on the stools beside him. He nearly took his beer and left, but he didn't feel like starting anything. The point of coming here was to drink in peace, have a couple more at home later on and black out for the night.

"What can I get you guys?" The bartender asked once she stopped wiping the counter, her hand coming over to rest on her jutted out hip.

The first guy leaned forward across the bar with a wry smile.

"Got any more sisters?"

His friends let out roaring laughs, slapping at their laps as they egged on their friend.

"Mike, you read my mind, brother," Big Tony belted out, his body still rumbling with amused laughter.

The bartender glared at them, her face twisting in annoyance.

Lonnie seemed to shrink into himself at her hard look, earning an annoyed scoff from Big Tony at his mild behavior.

"Three Buds and three shots of Cuervo," Lonnie muttered quietly.

The bartender nodded, her face slightly softening at his gentler tone. She turned to make their drinks, the noise soon picking back up.

"Oh yeah! Shake that ass, baby!" Lonnie shouted out, the words coming out forced. He looked at his friends with a hopeful look, like he was scrounging for their approval.

A tremor of anger shuddered up Danny's neck as he observed the scene quietly, his jaw continually tightening to the point that he thought that it would crack. He didn't understand how guys could be so outright raunchy and awful to women.

The bartender's face flushed a deep red as she struggled not to drop the shot glasses. She placed them on the counter before bringing over the beers, keeping her eyes down as she moved. She then poured the tequila into the shot glasses as the three men quieted down briefly. The tense nature of her body seemed to relax a little when they didn't say anything. As she moved to turn away, Big Tony shoved a five-dollar bill down the front of her blouse. She pried his hands off with a gasp, bewilderment exploding on her face as she stumbled back away from him.

"Treat the girl with some respect," Danny snapped at the three men as he whipped around on his stool, unable to keep quiet for another second.

Brief silence filled the bar before Big Tony blinked his eyes in surprise at Danny.

"What did you just say to me?" he asked, a threat already accompanying his words.

A part of Danny regretted saying anything, knowing that he needed to keep himself out of more trouble than he had already put himself through. He looked away from the three men, staring into the glass of his beer instead.

"Just have your drinks and leave," he grunted quietly before taking a deep sip of his.

Lonnie leaned over to have a closer look at Danny, a look of realization dawning on his sharp-featured face.

"Hol' up ... you're Danny Vitello, right?"

Danny found himself wishing that he could say no and claim to be another person. It wasn't a good time to be Danny Vitello, but he nodded regardless, knowing it would be harder to convince the man otherwise.

"Yeah," he uttered, refusing to look up.

The guys laughed among themselves, nudging each other as Big Tony smirked.

"You look a lot smaller in person," he told Danny, giving him a look over before turning to the bartender, who was still huddled back as far as she could be from them.

"Hey, honey. Put his drinks on our tab. He can't pay shit anyway," Big Tony laughed out.

Danny kept a straight face, despite feeling incredibly stung at the comment. Even if he was in the hole, he could still buy himself a few beers.

"I'm good," he grumbled with a shake of his head, wishing the men would leave him alone.

Mike leaned over to look at Danny, giving him a pointed look.

"Pretty boy, my friend here is just being nice. Why you gotta be like that?" he asked, grabbing at Danny's shoulder.

Danny nearly flinched at the touch, something immediately setting off inside of him. He felt it burn through his body, his right hand gradually forming a tight fist. Maybe it was the wasted audition or Max's short message to him that made him snap, or maybe he was just looking for more trouble to get into.

Danny's hand reached out for the closest one, his fingers digging into Big Tony's collar as he let his fist collide against his face in an unforgiving hit.

Mike scrambled to try to pry Danny off, but his arm was twisted back, and a sharp cracking noise sounded in the room as he wailed in pain.

Big Tony stumbled to his feet, his hand lifting to grab at his bleeding nose.

"What's your fucking problem, man!"

Danny glanced down at his fist, which was shaking, his chest feeling tight. He shouldn't have done that, and he knew that he was going to pay for it when Lonnie slammed his beer glass against Danny's head, sending him tumbling to the floor as all three descended on him.

Chapter Five

The first time that Danny was hauled off to jail, he was able to bust out using his superpowers, but that was all filmed on a studio lot. Today, a bright Thursday morning, he found himself sitting on a hard bench in an actual jail, surrounded by four other men that donned the same tired and annoyed expression as his. They all looked a little rough, and Danny couldn't help but feel ashamed for fitting in with such a group.

His black T-shirt was ripped at the neck, while droplets of blood stained his jeans and the tops of his sneakers. A distinct throbbing sensation echoed throughout the side of his face, which had been hastily bandaged. His nose ached, but he was fairly sure that it wasn't broken, luckily. Despite that, he didn't feel lucky at all. He was a wreck, and he kept dragging himself down. At this point, he would be dragging himself through and underneath rock bottom.

Heavy boots thumped against the floor toward the cell, and Danny straightened up with a hopeful look. A buzz loudly sounded as a burly cop stopped in front of the cell, motioning for Danny as he reached out to open the door.

"You made bail, Vitello," the cop grunted out.

Danny narrowed his eyes a little in confusion, but he remained quiet. At least he was able to get out of here. That was all that mattered at that point. He stopped at the front window to face a desk sergeant, who had a lean frame with a pointed face and sharp, watchful eyes. He reminded Danny of a hawk and further encouraged him to hurry up and get out of there.

The desk sergeant placed a Ziplock bag full of Danny's items on the desk, his eyes moving up to stare at Danny intently.

Keeping his own eyes down and away from the desk sergeant's, Danny retrieved his watch, phone, army dog tags, *Dodgers* cap, and keys. He watched the cop bend down and collect a form from a file cabinet before shoving it in front of Danny.

"Sign near the two X's," he said, his voice sounding gruff as he pointed at the line.

Danny grabbed a nearby pen and signed it before slipping his filthy cap on, lowering the brim over his eyes before shoving his things into his pockets.

"That's the exit on your right," the cop told him, nodding to a door.

Danny quietly nodded as he started to walk that way before the cop's voice halted him in his steps.

"Hey, Danny, mind if I get a selfie with ya?"

Danny clenched his jaw tightly, forcing his expression to remain neutral as he turned to face the cop, who already had his phone out. Internally, Danny was cringing, wishing that he was home right now. He used to love this sort of thing, but he wasn't someone to be admired now.

"Maybe another time, okay?" he replied, motioning to his busted up face. He didn't need that image circulating around the Internet.

"Come on, man," the cop pressed even more.

Danny blinked in shock at the guy's nerve, unable to keep himself calm and collected anymore.

"Seriously?" Danny sighed before shaking his head and trudging toward the exit quickly.

"Thanks for nothing, Mr. Has-Been. See you on *Dancing with the Stars*," the cop laughed out, making Danny pause to look back at him.

Danny felt that familiar tingle of anger, but he glanced around, noting that he could be shoved back in that jail cell before he was able to land a punch. It wasn't worth it. He drew in a deep breath before heading outside through the side door of the police station. His eyes squinted against the harsh glare of the sun, a feeling of discomfort and shame settling on him. He couldn't believe what he had gotten himself into. With just a few bucks left in his wallet, he knew that it was time to finally call someone. He lifted his left hand to shade his eyes as he turned to head down the sidewalk before a voice called out to him from behind.

"Danny," the voice called softly and nearby.

Danny stiffened at the familiar voice, his heart rate jumping up so rapidly that it nearly ached him. He turned around slowly, his eyes gradually widening.

"Angie," he breathed out, staring into the darkness of her sunglasses, which shielded the enchanting blue of her eyes that he briefly wished he could see. She looked incredible with her blonde curls tucked into a sun hat, her sleek legs on display in black shorts, and her slim body adorned in a sleeveless, flowery blouse. They were in two very different places.

"Rough night?" Angie asked as she slid her sunglasses off to survey him, a frown crossing her lips.

Danny felt more shame cover him like a dark cloud, making him wish that the ground would open beneath him. However, he was stuck there, so he opted for gruff pride to make him seem less pathetic.

"What are you doing here?" he asked, his eyes darting around to avoid her eyes. He didn't want to get lost in them. He already felt weak enough.

"Markus called me," Angie replied, her eyes still studying him intently.

Danny tried not to squirm beneath her gaze, wishing that she would look away. He knew that she wasn't impressed with what she saw.

"Figures," Danny said with a shake of his head.

"Don't be mad at him. He's shooting in Toronto and couldn't wire the bail money, so he called me," Angie replied, holding her hands up innocently.

"Well, I'll pay you back every cent," Danny bit out.

"What's your problem, Danny?" Angie sighed, her face softening.

Danny scoffed and shook his head, not wanting her to feel sorry for him. He wasn't a charity case.

"I don't need you doing me any favors, okay?" he told her with a firm voice.

Angie bit the corner of her lip.

"I see someone still has a chip on their shoulder," she commented lowly.

"That's rich coming from you," Danny snapped at her, unable to calm his tone. She was striking every sensitive nerve in his body, and he wasn't prepared for this. He didn't know how to handle her anymore after what she did to him.

"You always blame everyone else for your problems, Danny,"

Danny gave her a shocked look, his eyebrows lifting as he stared at her.

"In case you've forgotten, my so-called problems started when I walked into your trailer."

Angie shook her head, her eyes narrowing a degree.

"No, it began way before that, and you know it!" Angie stated firmly. She took a step closer to him, lifting her head to gaze deeply into his eyes.

"Where are you, Danny?" She nearly whispered the words, searching his eyes for something that Danny wasn't sure that she would find anymore.

"I'm right here," he stated.

A long curl slipped from her hat, falling against her forehead as she shook her head.

"No, you're not," she said, lowering her head as she tucked the loose strand back into place. She looked broken and disappointed, her frown refusing to leave her plush lips.

Danny couldn't stand her pitied look, and he shifted his eyes away from her. He understood that there was much to be disappointed about regarding his life, but she was the last person that he wanted pity from. It was ironic for sympathy to come from her after all that had happened between them.

"Huh?" he asked, trying to figure out what she meant.

Angie gestured to the jail he had just walked out of before pinching the bridge of her nose briefly.

"Whatever's going on with you … it's destroying your life. Have you seen anyone yet?" Angie asked, an expectant look crossing her face.

Danny shrugged, looking down at the ground without answering. What could he say to her? He had been scraping by the last year, and everything continued to get worse and worse. There was no way out of this.

"That's what I thought," Angie sighed to herself, her voice breaking as she stepped even closer to him. Her hand reached out, and he watched her place it gently on his elbow.

Danny nearly flinched away from the touch, his eyes narrowing at the contact. She hadn't touched him in forever, and every memory of her doing so threatened to flood back to his mind. He fought against them, feeling a distinct ache in his chest where his heart was. He wished that she could feel how much she was hurting him just by being there.

"If I knew how to take your pain away, I would. Please talk to someone," Angie urged him quietly, her voice unable to strengthen itself further. She lifted her hand to drift her fingertips along his cheek, her eyes shining a degree as she gazed at him softly.

Danny found himself leaning into her touch, despite his thoughts telling him to pull away, to get as far away from her as possible. She hurt him in ways that he would never recover from, yet he was letting her touch him, feel him.

"Bye, Danny," Angie told him before pulling her hand away and walking back down the sidewalk away from him. Her head tilted down in a saddened manner, her shoulders slumping as she got farther and farther away from him.

Danny's eyes trailed her until she turned the corner and was lost to his eyes. He drew in a steadying breath, hardly able to process what just happened. She had managed to walk herself right back into his life and then walk right back out just like that. How could she do that? Why would she do that? Questions upon questions clashed in his head, adding on to the overwhelming noise that already resided there.

Shaking his head in disbelief, Danny headed the opposite way, turning the corner to walk in front of the police station, but his path was cut off by several paparazzi lingering by the entrance. They surged forward toward him, snapping photos and shoving recorders in his face before he could react.

"Danny! What happened last night?" one shouted at him.

"Come on, Danny, what was it this time?" another paparazzi called out.

Danny covered his face with his hands as best as he could before hustling away, darting across a busy intersection and turning down a street. Danny maintained his quickened pace, taking turns almost at random for a few blocks until he was convinced that the paparazzi had finally given up their chase.

Danny slowed, panting out of exhaustion, but he continued to walk, still wanting to put as much distance between him and the paparazzi as possible. It would do him some good to walk and think anyway. He didn't need to waste what little money that he had left on a cab, and he had plenty of trouble on his mind that he needed to sort through. It was all a disaster. Danny grimaced, spotting a folded-up soda can on the ground. With an angered huff, he swung his foot at it to give it a kick, but he missed by a long shot.

"One of those days, eh friend?" a raspy voice sounded up ahead of him.

Danny looked down to see a homeless man sitting against a building. He was missing both legs and had a wheelchair beside him with a little dog tied to it. The skimpy dog lifted his head to look over at Danny in curiosity.

Beside the homeless man was a faded cardboard sign that read: "Homeless Vet. Anything Helps."

"I'd ask you for money, but I see you're not doing too well, eh, scrapper?" The older man grinned slightly, tapping his own cheek to gesture to Danny's injured one.

"Oh … yeah," said Danny, feeling bad for the man. Danny was bad off himself, but he knew that it could be worse. However, he was aware of how close he was to living on the street as well. Times were rough, and he questioned how long he would survive in them at this rate.

"Go to war overseas, and they don't do shit for us," the man remarked bitterly before reaching over to pat his dog on the head.

"True enough," Danny agreed, giving the man a sorry look before walking past him down the sidewalk. A year ago, he could've changed that man's life, giving him money to help get him off the street. Now, Danny was powerless in every way possible. He couldn't even help himself, which meant that he needed to call someone who could. Deciding to sleep off the pain echoing throughout his body first, Danny made his way through the city to his apartment, knowing that when he woke up, it would be time to call a lawyer.

The last thing that Danny wanted to deal with today was having to go to the L.A. county court. Sharply dressed lawyers strode from place to place as young receptionists and assistants darted through the hallways, their arms full of folders and papers. Everything seemed to be moving so quickly, while he had to drag himself through the building. He had decided to wear a navy blue blazer over a white button-down shirt and dark jeans, trying to dress somewhat nicely to make up for the fact that his face was still bruised around his nose and there was a bandage on his cheek. His body still ached with each step, but it was manageable for him. He just wanted to get this over with.

The lobby of the building was a chaotic nightmare for him to get through as journalists lunged at him with microphones and questions about his case. There wasn't much that he could tell them. He didn't even have an actual lawyer to represent him because he hadn't been able to afford one. It was a hard blow to him, ramping up his anxiety as he opted for government representation instead. It was the only thing that he could do besides represent himself, and that wouldn't pan out well.

Danny had not even met his public defender yet, which only made his nervousness about the case worse. He could only hope that they were good at their job and would work their hardest to keep him out of prison. The thought of going there had completely wrecked his sleep schedule, granting him a few restless nights. However, that wasn't all that bad to him. Less sleep meant fewer nightmares for him to suffer through, with which he was perfectly fine. He didn't need the added stress, especially after seeing Angie.

Running into Angie had flooded his mind with old memories, ones that he tried to hide in the back of his mind as much as he possibly could. If he turned his eyes to the past, he was afraid that he would never look forward. Times used to be so great, and then they disappeared in a rapid flash, leaving him feeling miserable in the present.

While he was suffering, she was excelling in her own life, which it seemed like she had pieced together perfectly. He was aware of how highly rated her movies were and of her budding fanbase. She rode the publicity blowout that sent him right to the bottom, capitalizing on the attention to take that wave all the way to the top.

Danny couldn't help but wonder if her concern for him was actually serious. She wanted him to talk to someone so badly, but why should he?

Why did she care? Him getting the help that she wanted him to wouldn't do anything to benefit her. He would still have to drag himself out of the hole if he ever could, while she hung around at the top, looking down on him from above. It just didn't make sense, and he wouldn't dare believe that she still had a smudge of love for him. He couldn't think about that. He couldn't think about her at all.

Once he slipped past the press and found his courtroom, Danny stepped inside, walking past the many sets of wooden pews that reminded him of the Sunday services he used to attend as a kid. He couldn't remember the last time that he had stepped foot in a church that wasn't a mock set at a studio. As the time for his case to start approached, he realized that he probably should've attended church more often.

As Danny approached, his gaze landed on a head of thin, gray hair, which belonged to a man hunched over a table on the defendant's side. Danny mouthed a quick prayer to the big guy upstairs before stepping up to his public defender and lightly tapping him on the shoulder.

The older man gave Danny a big smile, exposing cigarette-stained teeth. A tiny goatee rested on his chin, while acne scars and wrinkles adorned the rest of his aged face. His brown suit jacket was old and needed pressing, and his light blue tie had spots of dried coffee on it. He reached his hand out to Danny.

"Mr. Vitello, I'm Thomas Walker. It's an honor to meet you," he spoke excitedly, shaking Danny's hand in an energetic manner that didn't match his age.

"You too," Danny responded before taking his hand away and sitting down in one of the wooden chairs behind the table. He wasn't feeling very optimistic about his representation, but it was too late to really do anything about it now. Maybe this guy would surprise him, but Danny didn't get his hopes up.

Thomas sat down in the chair beside him and shuffled through the paperwork on the desk, grasping one page to glance at it.

"So, this isn't your first assault charge," Thomas commented.

Danny kept his eyes from rolling, having already known about his past. He didn't need to be reminded of that incident. He just wanted to know how this case would go without being taken down memory lane.

Thomas hummed beneath his breath as his eyes trailed down the length of the page, scanning the words.

"I see an incident of reckless driving, road rage … you could be facing some real time," Thomas sighed as he placed the sheet of paper down on the surface of the desk.

A jolt of panic struck Danny as he blinked his eyes a few times in surprise, not expecting to hear Thomas say that. He expected a fine or something along those lines, but he didn't want to go to prison.

"They jumped me! It was three against one! What was I supposed to do?" Danny defended himself with a firm shake of his head. He needed people to know the truth. Those guys had jumped him and beat him up, but he was the one facing serious time? It wasn't fair.

Thomas frowned as he listened to Danny, his own head slightly shaking.

"Not according to the bartender and the customers. They gave the cops a very different version," Thomas informed him.

Danny couldn't mask the shock that he felt hearing that, his jaw dropping open.

"The bartender? You've got to be kidding me!" Danny grumbled as he leaned back in his chair, pissed. He rubbed his hand over his face before pinching the bridge of his nose, feeling overwhelmed at all of this information. He couldn't believe that the bartender had sold him out like that after he had tried to spare her from the torment of those three animals. He expected her to be on his side, but he was obviously wrong.

"What's real time? Weeks? Months?" Danny asked, needing to know what he was possibly facing. He figured that he could suffer through a few weeks or so in prison. Maybe he could even get out early if he behaved well. He just didn't want to be in there longer than a few months. He had a life that he was trying to get together, and prison wouldn't look good on him. However, if Martha Stewart could do it and come back strong, so could he.

Thomas avoided Danny's eyes as he shrugged his shoulders and glanced at another piece of paper.

"Years!?" Danny asked, his words coming out faint as terror gripped him. It couldn't possibly be years. He only had a few charges, and his latest one was completely unrelated to his past ones. It was just a bad day. They had to understand that it was an isolated incident.

Thomas made a low clicking sound with his teeth as he shifted in his chair, throwing a quick glance at the room over his shoulder before looking back at Danny.

"That depends. This judge is pretty tough, but it's the prosecutor, Maria Toro, that I'm worried about. She's a real hard ass. They call her the 'The Bull'," he stated, sticking two fingers up to represent bull horns.

Danny let out a sigh as he shook his head, not believing how awful his luck was right now.

"Just freaking great," he fumed, his optimism taking a sharp plummet. "Look, I just want to plead guilty and get this over with." His eyes then shifted up as the judge walked in from his chambers.

The judge was in his mid-sixties with pasty-looking skin, a bald head, and a permanent scowl on his face. He stepped up behind his podium, his black robe flowing around him as he seemed to loom over the entire courtroom.

"All rise! The court is now in session. The honorable Judge Steven Jacoby presiding," the bailiff called out, his voice booming through the courtroom.

Danny rose to his feet with the rest of the courtroom. He could hardly believe that he was here again, but trouble trailed him as closely as his own shadow did. When the judge settled in his chair and the bailiff called for everyone else to sit, Danny eased himself back into his chair.

As Judge Jacoby flicked through the files before him about Danny's case, Thomas slowly stood from his seat.

"Your Honor?" he inquired, his voice coming out faint compared to the bailiff's.

Judge Jacoby peered over his square reading glasses, his mouth forming a straight line as his expression didn't waver.

"After speaking with my client, he's ready to plead guilty to the charges and accept full responsibility," Thomas told the judge as he clasped his hands together in front of him.

Judge Jacoby took one look at Danny before scowling and shaking his head in a disappointed manner.

"Your client has gone from being a regular on the movie screen to a regular at county lock-up," the judge's voice boomed throughout the courtyard, striking Danny hard as his quip made the audience chuckle.

Thomas sat down, looking like he had just been kicked.

"For the prosecution, Ms. Toro," the judge spoke, turning his head to gaze at a beautiful Hispanic woman in her thirties.

Maria Toro radiated confidence, even coming off bolder than the judge himself. She tilted her head up, her black hair flowing down her back as a black pantsuit and three-inch heels adorned her fit and trim body. She was a shark in blood-tainted water.

"Brace yourself," Thomas warned to Danny, who gazed at Maria in horror.

"Your Honor, after viewing the case, I recommend that the defendant be released on his own recognizance with two hundred hours of community service," Maria spoke loudly and clearly, her straight face not wavering as she faced the judge.

Judge Jacoby's eyebrows lifted in surprise, not expecting such a response from her.

Danny released the breath that he didn't even know he had been holding, his eyes shooting to Thomas, who leapt to his feet.

"Your Honor, my client and I are in total agreement with the prosecution's recommendation," Thomas announced with an enthusiastic nod.

Judge Jacoby turned back to Maria, giving her a confused look.

"That seems a little light considering his record, Ms. Toro," he told her, hinting for an explanation behind her words.

Maria nodded, her hands joining together in front of her.

"Your Honor, the defendant's attorney presented me with his client's military records. He is a Silver Star recipient, and he served two tours in Afghanistan and Iraq ..." Maria's words trailed off into a brief pause as her eyes moved sideways to catch Danny's, a tense moment happening between them before she spoke again to the judge.

"That should count for something," she finished with a faint nod.

Judge Jacoby fixed his gaze on Danny, a slight smirk adorning his lips.

"Well, Mr. Vitello, it's your lucky day. The court is not usually this lenient," the judge informed him.

Danny felt his heartbeat start to slow back down to its normal pace when he realized that he wasn't actually about to go to prison. He had somehow dodged that bullet, and it was all thanks to who he originally thought was his enemy. The tables had completely turned on him, and he was far happier with this outcome than the one that he had previously imagined.

"You will complete two hundred hours of community service ... make that "monitored" community service," Judge Jacoby added before giving Danny a stern glance, his jaw setting itself a bit tightly.

"Do not let me see you back in my courtroom. If you screw up once more, I promise you that you will do time," he told Danny firmly.

Danny sucked in a steadying breath as he fervently nodded, knowing not to cross this judge, who seemed to have it out for him.

"Thank you, Your Honor," Danny stated firmly, meeting the judge's eyes briefly before glancing down at the desk as the court began to transition for the next case. He closed his eyes briefly, thanking every being and power out there that had granted him this. He could hardly believe it, but he wasn't in handcuffs right now. He finally opened his eyes and glanced toward the right, catching Maria's eyes yet again.

Maria flashed him an encouraging smile before ducking her head and packing her files into her open suitcase.

"Come on," Thomas encouraged Danny, who broke his gaze from Maria reluctantly.

Danny looked forward and followed Walker out into the hallway, his eyes threatening to look back. He wondered why she took it so easy on him. Was she that awed by his military service? He couldn't help but wonder if it was something else that had swayed her decision. She could've easily pushed for him to be carted off to prison for a few weeks at least, especially since the judge seemed to respect her so highly.

"That will go down as one of my easiest cases ever. At a point, she was defending you better than I was!" Thomas admitted as he shook his head out of disbelief.

"So, what now?" Danny asked, wondering if this was it. He hoped that it was, because the judge did not want to see his face ever again. 200 hours of community service would take him forever, but at least he wouldn't be behind bars.

"Oh, it's pretty simple from here on out. You report to your assigned community service, and the monitoring officer will take care of the rest," Thomas replied with a faint shrug.

Danny parted his lips to reply until he spotted Maria heading out of the courtroom, his words getting caught in his throat. As Thomas started to stick his hand out for a handshake, Danny moved forward to trail Maria, who was heading toward the elevator. He couldn't let her disappear without them saying a word to each other. He needed to know why she did what she did and who she was, questions upon questions gathering in his mind. He cut her path off, his breath getting caught in his throat when he got close to her. She was even more stunning up close.

"Hey, I just wanted to say thank you," he told her as he stuffed his hands into his pants pockets. He felt a shudder of anxiety pass through him as they stood so close together, the smell of her perfume nearly dizzying him in the best way.

Maria tossed her hair back, drawing the dark strands away from her face, which harbored a slight smirk.

"Mhm," she replied casually as her eyes trailed over him briefly, like she was inspecting him.

Danny's anxiousness only doubled under her determined gaze, but he pushed on. He had captured her attention, but he needed to keep it. She seemed like a busy woman, and he didn't want to waste her time. She started walking briskly, prompting him to follow quickly.

"I'm kinda surprised because word around here ..." Danny trailed off awkwardly, cutting himself off when he realized that she probably wouldn't take being called "The Bull" lightly, and the last thing that he wanted to do was irritate her. He knew that the case was wrapped up and the sentence wouldn't change, but he still didn't want a woman like that harboring a grudge against him.

Maria paused, her steps stopping as she turned to face him with a curious look on her face.

"What word?" she asked, tilting her head a little.

Danny nearly squirmed on the spot, knowing that he needed to come up with something quickly because he couldn't backtrack his words. He cleared his throat awkwardly as he shuffled from foot to foot.

"Well ... that you're tough but fair," Danny explained with a faint laugh, hoping to lighten the mood. There was still tension between them, but he didn't know what it was just yet.

Maria hummed beneath her breath before she nodded and continued walking until she reached the elevator, her finger pressing the button with the arrow pointing upward.

Danny was starting to feel like a bumbling moron, heat flushing across his face as he stood next to her. He wanted to talk to her, but he just couldn't calm himself enough to properly speak to her. It was irritating.

"Well, I really appreciate what you did for me today," he managed to tell her, giving her a grateful look. Without her, he would be facing a much harsher sentence.

Maria swayed a little on the spot, waiting for the elevator doors to slide open.

"Yeah, you said that already, but I didn't do it for you," she replied evenly.

"Right," Danny automatically replied before his eyes widened as he processed what she just said to him.

"Wait, what?" he asked for clarification, feeling even more confused now. It was like he was trying to make himself look like an idiot at this point.

Maria shrugged, her eyes trailing down to the floor briefly. It was the most vulnerable that he had ever seen her look, but it was brief. She soon straightened up, lifting her chin as she spoke.

"Let's just say that I've experienced … seen cases like yours before. You might think that I saved you today, but the only thing that will save you in the future is yourself, Mr. Vitello," Maria told him as the elevator dinged and the doors slid open. She gave him a small nod before stepping into the elevator, the doors sliding shut between them.

Danny stood there for a minute, pondering on her words. He had heard part of them before from different people. He was his only saving grace, but he was obviously awful at that. He couldn't help but be self-destructive, to chain himself to the bottom so that he could never be as happy and successful as he used to be. He didn't know what he had against himself to keep doing that, but it wasn't going away any time soon. No one could change that, not her or Angie.

At the thought of Angie, Danny grimaced, shaking himself from his thoughts as he headed out of the county courthouse. He needed some fresh air and a walk, and his steps took him down the street toward his apartment. At least he could go home. Earlier, he had thought that he wouldn't be able to do that before Ms. Toro stepped in and saved his skin.

At this point, he was ready for today to be over. He wanted to have a few beers and watch television until he fell asleep. That was all that he wanted for the rest of the day. Once he got back to his apartment and stepped inside, he looked down to see his cat rubbing up against his ankles happily.

"I missed you, too, Buddy. You know that I could never leave you," Danny told him, smiling at his cat as he leaned down to scratch Buddy between his ears. Another downside to going to prison would have been leaving Buddy, though he would have made sure his precious cat was in someone else's care while Danny was gone.

Danny started to head to his bedroom to get changed out of his court clothes and into a shirt and shorts, but he heard knocking on his front door. Narrowing his eyes in confusion, Danny turned back around and opened the door to see Mr. Baccala standing there.

Mr. Baccala rubbed at the back of his neck awkwardly, his eyes resting on Danny's shoes instead of his battered face.

"The wife say we cannot do this no more," he stated uncomfortably.

Danny stared at Mr. Baccala in surprise, his heart rate picking back up at the announcement.

"But I asked for the rest of the month," Danny pointed out, having thought that this wasn't an issue anymore.

"She see you with black eye again … she fear you will bring gang around," Mr. Baccala explained with a shake of his head. "You know, women, eh?" Mr. Baccala added as he gave Danny an uncomfortable smile, finally meeting his eyes.

Danny stiffened, countless words coming to his mind to say that might convince Mr. Baccala to let him stay, but he didn't say a single one. He knew that it wouldn't matter. What was done was done.

"I'll be out tomorrow," Danny told him, dread filling him. He hadn't expected this to happen so soon, and he was far from prepared for this.

"I … really sorry, Danny," Mr. Baccala sighed, giving Danny a guilty look.

"Thank you, Mr. Baccala. You're a good man," Danny told him, not wanting him to feel bad. It hadn't been his decision.

Mr. Baccala gave Danny a faint nod before shuffling back down the hallway.

Danny shut the door behind him and reached for his phone, knowing what he needed to do. He had nowhere else to turn to at this point, and he wouldn't dare subject Buddy to living out on the street with him. With a disappointed shake of his head, and with nowhere else to turn, he called Markus.

Chapter Six

Markus Moore was an African American man in his mid-sixties, but his shoulders had the build of a football player, which was fitting since he had played college ball at Alabama University until he busted a knee. Despite his age, hardly any wrinkles adorned his face, except for when he laughed, when a few fine lines appeared beneath his eyes. The only way for someone to tell that he was older were the gray streaks in his hair. He was the closest thing that Danny had to a father and a best friend. They hadn't seen each other since Danny's life started spiraling out of control. Now, he stood outside his house, nervous and embarrassed.

Danny paused at Markus's front door in this upscale neighborhood of Sherman Oaks, his eyes sweeping over the oak-paneled door. He lifted his hand to knock, but he stopped, hating that it had to come to this. His bags were at his feet, and Buddy was relaxed in a cat carrier held securely in his left hand. He didn't want to see Markus like this.

Before he could make up his mind, Lydia, Markus's wife, swung the door open and beamed at him. She was petite and smiling, her eyes twinkling as the light brown of her skin seemed to glow. She was always like this, a beacon of optimism, and Danny couldn't help but be envious of how she saw the world around her.

"Danny! There you are!" welcoming him happily before launching her small frame right into his arms.

Danny caught her and held her, inhaling her comforting hug he so missed these past years. For that moment, he felt the world tilt back to normal.

"Hi, Lydia," he greeted her warmly as they parted from each other.

"Come inside!" Lydia invited as she reached forward to grab Buddy's carrier from him. She led him inside of the house toward the living room, where Markus stood with his arms wide open.

"Look, our boy is finally here," Lydia said, as Danny walked up to Markus, where they embraced strongly. Lydia carrying Buddy toward another room.

"Come on, Buddy. Let me show you around," she cooed to the cat as she left.

"We've been worried sick about you these past two years, I called you, I wrote" Markus whispered, and then took off his glasses to wipe his eyes tearing up with joy.

"I know, Markus" Danny sincerely replied. "I was… in a bad place." Danny said, while his own eyes welled up.

Once they parted, Markus inspected Danny's marked up face, his comforting look wavering a little at the sight.

"Dang! Looks like you were in the octagon with Anderson Silva," Markus commented, eyeing the bruising on Danny's face.

Danny reached up to tentatively touch his face, a weak laugh breaking from him. He was aware that he didn't look all that great.

"Feels like it, too. It's really good to see you, Markus. I appreciate you guys letting me crash here. I won't be here long. I promise," Danny replied, giving Markus a grateful look. If it wasn't for Markus, Danny had no idea what he would do. He didn't have any connections or fallbacks as he used to. It felt like it was just him and Buddy against the world.

Markus waved his hand dismissively before patting Danny on the shoulder.

"Danny, you're family. You know that. Stay as long as you need to," Markus told him.

Danny sighed as he hung his head, looking defeated.

"Money's been tight, the IRS took everything, just some residual checks coming in and ..." Danny started to explain until Markus held up his hand and cut him off.

"What did I just tell ya?" Markus said pointedly before leading Danny over to the couch. He plopped down where he had been sitting before, his head nodding to the spot next to him for Danny to sit.

Danny thanked him quietly before lowering himself down on the couch, his eyes falling on a pile of photos that were sprawled out on the coffee table in front of the couch.

"What's all this?" Danny asked, a confused look appearing on his face as he glanced over at Markus.

Markus leaned forward to gaze down at the photos.

"Lydia gathered these up this morning. You and me, our first movie together after ya got back," Markus explained.

Danny reached forward to pick up a few of the photos to inspect them, memories rushing back to his mind.

"Seems like yesterday I was getting to work with the Mighty Markus Moore. I was only *slightly* nervous," Danny joked, reminiscing aloud and coaxing a laugh from the both of them. "I called Max ... was hoping he'd rep me again. He basically told me to get lost. No one's interested," Danny admitted with a shake of his head. He wished that someone would just take a chance on him.

"Man, that's hogwash. You were his biggest client!" Markus scoffed.

Danny laughed bitterly as he sat back against the couch.

"I used to be his only client at one time."

Markus quietly shook his head.

"Tell you what, I can get you in with my guy at Global. He's been doing great things for me," Markus offered after nudging Danny.

"I noticed. I saw your billboard on Ventura Blvd," Danny replied with a little smile. He knew that he could count on Markus to help him out.

"Nice, huh? One over on Sunset, too," Markus beamed in a proud manner.

Danny laughed and patted Markus's shoulder, feeling happy for his friend. Even if his own life wasn't going all that well, he still wanted to show his support for his successful friends. He knew how hard it was to get out there and make it.

"Glad to have you back in our lives, Danny boy. And Lydia ... she's happier than a butcher's dog," Markus chuckled as he threw his arm around Danny's shoulders.

Danny smiled and leaned into the embrace, feeling better than he had in a long time.

Danny watched various buildings flit by through the window of the Uber that he rode in. He was heading out to do his community service, which he wasn't too stoked about, but it was better than being in jail. He felt the black sedan come to a stop, and his eyes landed on the Cedars-Sinai Medical Center just outside the window.

"Thanks," Danny said to the driver before getting out of the car and walking into the medical center, narrowing his eyes against the bright white interior. He made his way to the front desk to talk to the receptionist, who was sifting through paperwork. He cleared his throat, hoping to capture her attention.

"I'm supposed to meet the hospital administrator, Linda Schwartz?"

The receptionist, without looking up from the papers that she was organizing, responded, "And you are?"

"Danny Vitello."

The receptionist's head shot up, a look of recognition and surprise crossing her face.

"Oh my gosh, it is you! Hi! You can have a seat. I'll try to reach her," the receptionist replied as she gestured to the waiting area behind Danny.

"Okay, thanks," Danny replied before heading to the waiting area to sit down. He glanced around, noting that a few people in the waiting area recognized him and were pointing and whispering. He pretended not to notice, merely lowering his head a degree so that his bruises and black eye weren't all that visible.

After waiting for ten minutes, Danny finally found himself outside the administrator's office. He knocked on the door frame before peeking his head in, his eyes landing on an older woman with a stern face that had to be Linda Schwartz.

"Danny Vitello. I'm supposed to talk to you about community service," he introduced himself, waiting for her to wave him in, which she did, before asking him to take a seat at her desk across from her. He tried not to feel uneasy as her crisp blue eyes seemed to drill into him.

"Mr. Vitello, it isn't often we get a celebrity ordered to perform community service here, but you're not the first either," Linda commented in a pointed manner as she folded her hands in front of her delicately.

"Do the crime, do the time," Danny weakly chuckled, hoping to lighten the situation with some humor. It didn't work.

Linda gave him an unamused look, her lips pulling tight in a rigid line.

"Whatever you have in mind, I'm willing to do, ma'am," Danny told her, shifting back into serious mode before he got in trouble somehow.

"You're going to be with us for the next ..." Linda trailed off as she looked through a few papers on her desk. She looked back up at Danny with a hint of a judging look. "200 hours. Normally, we'd have you cleaning floors or bathrooms," she continued.

Danny fidgeted in his chair, guessing that she was going to give him an even worse task.

"But I was thinking of something more in line with your skills," Linda veered in a different direction than he was expecting.

"My skills?" Danny questioned, wondering where this was headed.

Linda nodded before continuing.

"Our Pediatrics staff puts on a play every year with the children. You could make this year's event top notch," Linda explained to him with a faint smirk on her lips.

Danny stared at her curiously, wondering if he actually heard her right or not. She wanted him to put on a play? He was an award-winning actor, and that was what she wanted him to do.

"You're kidding, right?" Danny asked, wondering if she was the one joking now.

Linda merely smiled sweetly at him.

"A play? Like a kid's play? With homemade costumes and all that?" Danny asked with a touch of skepticism, needing to know exactly what he was about to get into. It wasn't like he could back out.

"Yes. And all that," Linda quipped.

Danny shook his head, refusing to stoop so low. It felt like a jab to his reputation, and he had endured enough hits already.

"Oh, yeah, no, I don't think so," he replied.

"This is *monitored* community service, Mr. Vitello, and I'm the monitor. I could call the court and let them know you're declining your punishment. It's up to you," Linda told him with a half-hearted shrug, a wicked look crossing her face.

Danny sat there frowning, knowing that there was no way out of this for him. He was stuck, and she seemed to be finding all sorts of satisfaction in that.

"Fine!" Danny exclaimed, giving in. He just needed to get these 200 hundred hours of community service over with as soon as he possibly could.

"Good. Ms. Toro will be happy to know that you're on board," Linda replied.

"Toro? Like, 'The Bull'?" Danny asked, feeling his heartbeat jolt at that.

Linda met his gaze evenly, a half-smile quirking up on her lips.

"Toro, like the prosecutor."

After leaving the medical center, Danny found himself in an office at the VA in front of Dr. Vanowen, a man in his late sixties wearing glasses, a tan sweater, and a tweed jacket. Family photos in black frames littered his desk, while a Norman Rockwell painting of a doctor listening to a little girl's doll's heartbeat with his stethoscope hung on the wall behind him.

Dr. Vanowen pushed his thin-framed glasses up the sharp slope of his nose as he turned a few pages in Danny's records.

"What brings you to the VA today, Sergeant?" he asked without looking up from the pages.

Danny's eyes threatened to widen a little at the title, not having heard it in a long time.

"Wow, I haven't been called that in a while," he answered back, his eyes trailing along the surface of Dr. Vanowen's desk.

"Would you rather that I call you Danny?" Dr. Vanowen asked once he looked up at him.

Danny nodded, feeling the hair on the back of his neck stand up a little. There were too many harsh memories associated with his old military title, which he would prefer to forget.

"If you don't mind," Danny replied.

Dr. Vanowen nodded before sitting up straight and resting his forearms on the top of the desk.

"What brings you to the VA today, Danny?"

Danny swallowed hard, hardly knowing what to say. The decision to come here had been made on the fly because a swarm of thoughts and worries had been haunting him for so long. He could hardly stand the noise inside of his own mind anymore.

"I ... uh ... I need help. I've been ... things have been ... I'm just ..." Danny continued to stumble over his response, unable to properly express his own thoughts. He stopped talking for a few moments, his head shaking slowly in disappointment. How was he supposed to get help if he couldn't even describe why he needed help?

Dr. Vanowen held up a hand briefly, giving Danny a softer look.

"Take your time, son."

Danny nodded before drawing in a deep breath and starting once again.

"I'm finding life to be really hard. I'm having these dreams ... trying to cope with some anger ... trying not to remember things," Danny started to piece together some of his worries, highlighting the things that had been bothering him the most lately.

"You were discharged almost ten years ago. I'm sure you're familiar with the term PTSD?" Dr. Vanowen asked.

Danny nodded his head, figuring he had some sort of degree of that. It would explain some of the things that he had been going through.

Dr. Vanowen cleared his throat.

"Have you ever wanted to hurt yourself, Danny?"

Danny stared at Dr. Vanowen for a few uncomfortable moments, silence hanging between them. That was a difficult topic for Danny, one that he didn't feel like talking about.

"We're only as sick as what we hide inside," Dr. Vanowen commented.

Danny stood up with a shake of his head, his fingers curling into tight fists as a wave of heat washed over him.

"I just want to feel like a normal person again ... to sleep ... and not be haunted by those images that keep playing over and over ... not to wake up in a pool of sweat," Danny nearly growled out, his narrowed eyes seeming to glaze over as he stared into empty space.

Dr. Vanowen took off his glasses as Danny spoke, studying him carefully.

"To not jump every time that I hear a car backfire," Danny continued, his voice growing quieter and weaker with each word that he spoke. His strength felt like it was being sapped just by talking about his experiences.

Danny shuddered, his eyes shifting to the ground as he moved to stand by the window, sunlight streaming across his face. However, he didn't feel any warmth.

"I just want it all to end," he said, his eyes drifting shut. Sometimes, the darkness was comforting to him, like the end he sometimes craved. It was peaceful, contrasting from the awful chaos that was his life currently.

"It's going to take some time, but we ..." Dr. Vanowen started to say.

"You don't know what it's like, okay! You have no fucking clue!" Danny snapped as he whipped around, unable to control the anger pumping through him like blood. He seethed quietly as silence fell on the room again, his narrowed eyes resting on Dr. Vanowen.

"I want to show you something," Dr. Vanowen said, breaking the silence as he turned to a shelf with hundreds of books. He reached forward to pull out an old school yearbook. He flipped through the pages until stopping on one, his gaze resting on the page for a little while before he turned the book to show Danny.

"That's me …" Dr. Vanowen said as he pointed to the page.

Danny moved closer to see the picture, a confused look crossing his face.

Dr. Vanowen rubbed his chin briefly, looking pained, before pointing to another person in the picture.

"That was the Monsignor of my parish," he added.

Danny looked at the picture closely before slowly dragging his gaze up to the doctor.

"He sexually abused me from fifth to eighth grade," Dr. Vanowen breathed out shakily, a frown crossing his lips.

"I'm sorry," Danny told him, giving the doctor a sympathetic look.

"Memories don't go away, Danny, but we can learn to manage them. PTSD isn't just a soldier problem. It's been around forever," Dr. Vanowen explained as he put a hand on Danny's shoulder in an empathetic manner.

"It takes time, son. We'll take it slow. I promise."

Danny nodded his head.

"We have to address what triggers certain memories, your interpretations of them," Dr. Vanowen told him.

Danny rubbed his hands on his legs, a tremor of terror shuddering through him at the thought. He didn't like going out of his way to think of those memories, but he knew that he needed to face them if he wanted to heal from their effects. He couldn't just let them haunt him forever and continue to ruin him. He had to take a stand against his own mind at some point.

Chapter Seven

"Wait here."

Danny nodded as he stood in one of the long hallways of the Cedars-Sinai Medical Center late in the afternoon, his eyes trailing Maria Toro as she walked into one of the hospital rooms with Nurse Sally, a 60-ish, heavy-set African American woman. The hospital felt cold all around him, and he still hadn't gotten used to that.

"Mom, you got back fast," a young boy's voice sounded from inside of the room.

"You have a visitor, Sam," Maria told him softly. Danny figured that was his cue to enter, prompting him to walk inside, his eyes falling on a frail boy in the hospital bed watching television. Despite looking weak and being covered in wired electrode pads with sensors from head to toe, the boy seemed to be in high spirits.

"Hey, you look like … no way! No way!" Sam gasped out once he saw Danny, his dark eyes immediately lighting up. He reached over to the side table near his bed to snatch up a purple-winged action figure. He glanced at it and then back at Danny, a few dark hairs falling against his forehead.

"Woah! The Purple Hawk!"

Danny hid a wince when he saw the thick gauze bandage on the side of Sam's head, along with all of the wires and machines hooked up to him. Sam was just a kid. He didn't belong in this place. He looked so small in the hospital bed, like the white sheets were swallowing him whole.

"Come on! Call me Danny," he told Sam with a warm smile as he approached Sam's bedside.

"Mom, is this really him?" Sam asked as he turned to look at Maria with starry eyes.

Maria nodded with a bright smile, happy wrinkles forming in the creases of her soft eyes.

Sam looked back at Danny, his eyes catching on to his hero's bruised face.

"You think my face looks bad, you should see the other guy's fists … that's one of your lines from …" Sam started to say in a deep voice.

"*The Troublemaker*. Wow. He knows my movies better than my last agent!" Danny chuckled upon hearing the familiar line, his eyes widening a little in surprise as Nurse Sally laughed.

"It's good to meet you, Sam. I brought you a little something," Danny told him as he handed Sam a movie script that he held in his hand.

"It's a bit worn, but this was my script from *The Purple Hawk vs. The World*," Danny explained, hoping that Sam would like it. Despite Sam seeming cheery, Danny could only imagine how much discomfort and pain the kid went through on a daily basis. Maria hadn't gone into detail about what was wrong with Sam, but Danny figured that it wasn't anything good.

"That's my *favorite* movie!" Sam gasped out excitedly as he flipped through the script.

"Yeah, your mom told me," Danny smiled as he glanced over at Maria. It was nice seeing her smile, which seemed to light up the entire room. He could tell that Sam was her world.

"Very kind of you, Mr. Vitello," Maria replied, giving Danny a smile back before turning her head to hide her expression behind her dark hair. Her hands moved to adjust the lapel of her black blazer over a white blouse, looking like she just came from the courthouse.

"This is so cool! Thank you! Look, Mom! It's autographed, too!" Sam exclaimed as he pointed to Danny's scrawled autograph in black Sharpie on the front page.

"That is pretty cool, huh?" Maria replied, giving her son a warm look.

"Check it out, Nurse Sally," Sam said, turning to his nurse.

"Very nice, Sam," Nurse Sally beamed happily at Sam as she clapped her hands together.

"Taking good care of Sam, Sally?" Danny asked her with a playful smirk.

"Doing the best that I can … but he's such a nuisance … causes me all kinds of problems," Nurse Sally stated, trying to keep a straight face but soon cracking into a laugh.

"Nuh uh! Not me. Nurse Sally just can't deal with me always beating her in poker," Sam argued with a wicked grin.

"He got me for five bucks last week," Nurse Sally proclaimed pointedly, narrowing her dark eyes slightly.

"You're in good hands, Sam," Danny chuckled.

Sam nodded his agreement before flipping through the script again to the best of his ability, his right hand harboring monitors.

Danny stared at Sam's EKG monitor, a small frown threatening to cross his lips.

"Giving up ain't an option," Sam said quietly.

Danny turned to Sam, a surprised look crossing his face after hearing such a profound statement come from the young boy.

"What?"

Sam held up the script that he was reading.

"Your line from the movie when the aliens were about to drop you into the volcano," Sam explained.

"Oh, right," Danny replied, remembering what scene Sam was talking about. His acting days seemed so long ago at this point.

"I say it before all of my treatments and operations," Sam declared as he lifted his chin proudly.

"I can vouch for that," Nurse Sally added as she reached up to pull her hair back tighter in her hair tie. Maria chimed in as well.

"He sure does! Well, I have to run home for a bit. I'll be back in an hour, Sam. I love you," Maria told her son before leaning over to peck his forehead affectionately.

"Love you, Mom," Sam told her with a smile.

Maria nodded at Danny briefly before leaving the room, Nurse Sally following behind her.

"I saw you on one of the news channels last week. They were pretty mean," Sam commented, breaking the silence that had filled the room for a moment.

"Yeah, well, I probably deserved it," Danny sighed, able to only guess what had been said about him. He hadn't done anything all that great or notable to be commended, so he could imagine that it was all negative.

"They said that your acting career was over. Is that true?" Sam asked, a frown crossing his face.

"I hope not! I mean, I made a lot of mistakes over the past few years," Danny explained, trying to figure out the best way to approach this topic with a ten-year-old. Sam seemed like a good listener, though, and he was smart.

"Everyone makes mistakes," Sam replied with a shrug.

Danny smiled a little at Sam's positivity, wishing that was the case, but not everyone made the mistakes that he had.

"I know, but I made mine while the whole world was watching. So, that kinda makes it a little tougher," Danny told him as he walked across the while tile of the room to the window, peering into the darkness outside through the white blinds. That was the cost of being a celebrity. Everything that he did, whether it was good or bad, was done in the spotlight for everyone to see.

"I've seen all of your movies, even the ones when you aren't *Purple Hawk*," Sam voiced.

Danny chuckled a little as he shook his head.

"I hope your parents don't let you watch *all* of my movies. You might be a little too young for a few of 'em," Danny told Sam as he turned away from the window to grin at the young boy.

Sam glanced back down at the script with a little shake of his head.

"It's just me and my mom. My dad died in the war. He was in the Army."

It felt like a brick landed on Danny's chest, nearly making it hard to breathe after hearing that. He frowned and rubbed at the back of his neck, feeling pain echo through his body and mind.

"Oh, I'm sorry to hear that, Sam. I bet he was a great guy," Danny said quietly, hoping that he hadn't upset Sam. He hadn't known that Sam's father had passed away. He just figured that he was out of the picture.

"He died before I was born," Sam replied as he looked back up at Danny.

"Well … your dad was a *real* superhero," Danny told him with a small smile. He fully knew about the struggles and sacrifice of being in the military, but it was a thought that he didn't want to reflect on too deeply. He still had plenty of open wounds from his own experience.

Sam brightened up at Danny's reply, coaxing him to nod.

"He sure was! My mom has all of his medals and his Army pictures and stuff above our fireplace," Sam told Danny in a proud manner, his chin even lifting up a little. His pride in his father was evident, and it warmed Danny's heart.

Before Danny could reply, Sam's doctor, Doctor Kumar, entered the room. He was in his fifties, dark skinned, middle eastern gentleman. His hair was dark and cut short, wearing black-framed glasses and a white lab coat over his suit.

"Hello, Sam. How are you feeling?" Doctor Kumar asked Sam in a cheery tone as he approached the boy's bedside.

Sam turned away from Danny to smile politely at his doctor.

"Hi, Doctor Kumar. I feel okay. This is my friend, Mr. Vitello … I mean, Danny," Sam introduced the two.

70

Doctor Kumar looked over at Danny, a look of recognition immediately crossing his face.

"Hello, Danny! My wife and I loved you in *The Devil's Deal*," he chuckled softly as he gestured to Danny, looking him up and down, like he was surprised that he was real.

"*The Deal with the Devil*," Sam corrected him pointedly.

Danny couldn't help but chuckle at Sam's knowledge of his films. It was nice to have such a devoted fan. It felt like he had lost his entire fanbase after everything that had happened, but he couldn't blame them for leaving. He really hadn't been someone to look up to lately.

"Oh, yes. Right. Great movie!" Doctor Kumar laughed out after facepalming himself at his mistake.

Sam thrusted his script up toward Doctor Kumar, like he had been waiting for the first opportunity that he could find to show it off.

"Look, Doctor Kumar, Danny brought me this," Sam told him with a toothy smile.

Doctor Kumar leaned close to inspect the script.

"Very nice, Sam! We loved that one, too. Any new movies coming out, Danny?"

Danny chuckled with a little shrug. "Funny you should ask. I'm gonna be directing and producing a big event. I'm helping Cedars put on its annual holiday show," Danny explained as the doctor gazed at him curiously, prompting a sudden gasp from Sam.

"Wait! Does that mean you're gonna be here a lot more? At the hospital?" Sam exclaimed, sitting up a little more in his bed, the sheets falling to his waist.

"Looks that way, Sam," Danny told him warmly. At least someone was glad to have him around.

"Awesome!" Sam cheered, pumping his fist in an excited manner that coaxed a laugh from his doctor.

"Yes, that is awesome," Doctor Kumar agreed with a nod.

Danny checked the time on the ticking clock on the wall in the room before clasping his hands together.

"Well, I should get going. Nice meeting ya, Doc. See ya soon, Sam," Danny bid them goodbye.

"Thanks for visiting, Danny! And thanks for the script!" Sam told him as he moved to stick out his hand to shake Danny's. However, with the monitor on his palm and the IV tube on top of his hand, he could only muster his pinky finger.

Danny smiled and wrapped his pinky around Sam's, locking them briefly in a small shake.

"Take care, kiddo," he replied before turning to head out of the room.

Sam beamed from ear to ear, his eyes trailing his idol as Danny walked away.

Danny headed down the hallway toward the elevator, listening to the soft thud of his shoes against the white tile. He didn't feel as eerie being here as usual. Maybe Sam had lightened his spirit some. He glanced over to see Nurse Sally huddled up near a desk with a few other nurses, and he lifted his hand in a wave.

"Bye, Nurse Sally. Oh, hey, can I ask you a question?" Danny halted his steps, unable to contain his curiosity.

Nurse Sally nodded and parted from the group of nurses to walk over to Danny, her friends nudging each other and smiling Danny's way.

"What can I do for you?" Nurse Sally asked him, cocking an eyebrow out of curiosity.

Danny politely smiled at the other nurses before turning to Nurse Sally.

"Sam told me he has ... um ... Medulla-something-toma?" Danny spoke in a hushed voice.

"Medulloblastoma. It's a cancerous tumor in his brain. They removed most of it last week," Nurse Sally explained to him.

Danny frowned, not liking the sound of his diagnosis.

"How long will he be here?" Danny asked, hoping that Sam could get out of the hospital soon. He should've been in school making friends or having fun somewhere.

"Recovery time is different for everyone. Could be a few days to a few weeks. He has the biggest heart of any child that I know ... everything he's been through ... he's coded twice," Nurse Sally sighed with a shake of her head, her hands disappearing into the pockets of her light blue scrubs.

"Coded?" Danny questioned, narrowing his eyes in confusion.

"His heart stopped. Twice," Nurse Sally explained, a grave look on her face.

Danny nearly flinched after hearing that, his wide eyes staring into the open space in front of him. It was hard to imagine that Sam's heart had stopped beating two separate times, but he still came back. He was still here and alive. That really was a miracle.

"That's ... I mean ... wow. Well, I better get going," Danny said quietly after drawing in a deep breath to settle himself. He was ready to get out of this place. It made him feel so heavy.

Nurse Sally placed a hand on his arm to keep him from walking away just yet.

"I heard that you'll be in charge of putting together our holiday play?"

Danny gave her a surprised look, not expecting her to know that.

"Word spreads fast around here," he commented.

Nurse Sally shrugged as she glanced back at her group of friends before looking back at him.

"Yes, it does. I watch the news and read the magazines ... so, don't screw up. These kids mean the world to me," she told Danny pointedly, her expression turning deadly serious.

She had a maternal vibe to her, one that told Danny not to mess with her or her kids unless he wanted to face the gravest of consequences. She walked away from him, leaving him stunned on the spot.

Chapter Eight

Tired huffs broke from Danny as he jogged alongside Markus on the track of one of the local high schools. They were finally finishing up their late morning run, and Danny was struggling to even pick his feet up off of the track at that point. He couldn't remember the last time that he had exercised.

"Dang! I'm out of shape," Markus puffed out as he slowed to a stop to lean over, placing his hands on his knees over his sweats.

"Aw, that wasn't so bad, old man," Danny breathed out with a weak chuckle, reaching out to pat his friend on the back.

"Hey, easy there," Markus smirked, playfully swatting at Danny as he straightened up and walked slowly at Danny's side.

"So, I spoke to my guy at Global … said he has a full stable right now … didn't think he'd be able to give you the attention you deserve," Markus sighed out, giving Danny an apologetic look as they circled the track that surrounded a thick, green field.

"Man, that's the best sugarcoating that I've ever heard you give," Danny chagrined, his eyes focusing on the tips of his tennis shoes. He honestly wasn't that surprised at this point. All that he had been faced with lately was disappointment.

"Sorry. All the bad press …" Markus remarked quietly.

"No worries. I'll figure it out. I got my work cut out for me the next few weeks putting this show together at Cedars. Come on, one more lap," Danny replied with a dismissive wave of his hand. He didn't want to think about any of that right now. He nudged Markus before taking off down the track, leaving Markus to shake his head before following.

Later that day after cleaning up after his run, Danny found himself back in Doctor Vanowen's office. Even if he didn't want to think about the troubles in his life, he knew that he needed to talk to someone about them. His mind didn't need to take any more damage than it already had.

"You did burn some bridges, Danny. It takes time …" Doctor Vanowen sighed as he sat across his cluttered desk from Danny, his hand adjusting the collar of his black sweater.

"I'm not looking for any favors," Danny stated blandly, staring down at his hands in his lap.

"Trust is earned. Make amends to people you've hurt. You said your ex-wife bailed you out, yet you couldn't even thank her. Why?" Doctor Vanowen asked him, tilting his head curiously.

Danny sank back into the padded chair that he was sitting in, his shoulders slumping slightly. This was territory that he was reluctant to venture into.

"Guess I still blame her for our breakup," Danny replied with a shrug.

"You think if she were the one experiencing depression and bursts of anger, you'd have been any better of a spouse than she was?" Doctor Vanowen asked.

Danny blinked a few times in surprise, feeling like Doctor Vanowen had punched him in the stomach instead of asked him a question.

"No," he managed to mutter.

"It could be cathartic to let her know your feelings. Maybe call her, or better yet, an email, laying it all out," Doctor Vanowen suggested calmly.

Danny quietly grinded his teeth a little, his eyes roaming the mess of papers and office supplies on Doctor Vanowen's desk. He couldn't look at his doctor right now as a storm overtook his mind.

"Yeah. I don't know. I'll have to think about that one," Danny said quietly, bringing the conversation to a swift end. He wasn't sure if he owed Angie anything. She had derailed him, broken him. He didn't even know what words he could spare on her. If he could remove her from his mind, maybe he would. At least a decent amount of the pain that haunted him would disappear, too.

In one of the stark white hallways at Cedars-Sinai Medical Center, Maria walked along the shiny tile, clutching her purse to her side. She glanced up to see Nurse Sally heading down the hallway toward her from the opposite direction.

"Good morning! We just brought Sam breakfast. His appetite is coming back. That's a great sign," Nurse Sally said cheerfully as she stopped in front of Maria.

"I'll take all of the good news I can get," Maria said with a relieved smile.

"Danny Vitello was here earlier. He's been putting those on every floor," Nurse Sally told her before pointing to a bulletin board on the wall next to them. In the middle of the bulletin board was a poster that read

"AUDITION SIGN UP! PETER PAN – Staff and Patients of Cedars-Sinai Hospital. Performance on December 24th."

Maria peered at the poster curiously, a small smile beginning to quirk up on her lips.

"Speak of the devil," Nurse Sally observed beneath her breath as she nudged Maria and then nodded toward the opposite end of the hall, where Danny was heading toward them from.

"I have patients to see. Bye," Nurse Sally chirped before walking away and leaving Maria alone as Danny approached.

"Checkin' out the flyer, huh? Sorry, only staff and patients are allowed to audition," Danny joked with her as he nodded to his poster, a smile playing out on his lips.

Maria smirked and shook her head. "I was just gonna go visit Sam before I have to get back to work. So, Peter Pan, huh?" Maria asked, lifting her eyebrow at him out of interest.

"One of my favorites," Danny told her, which was the main reason why he chose that theme. Plus, it was easy to pull a cast together for it.

"Mine too," Maria replied with a nod, awkward silence soon following her words as Danny chuckled faintly.

Unable to take the silence anymore, Danny cleared his throat as he scratched at the back of his neck above the collar of his white T-shirt.

"Hey … um … maybe we could get a coffee later or … dinner …" Danny stumbled over his words, his face burning a degree. He hadn't meant to sound like a bumbling fool, but it was too late to take any of that back now.

Maria's face hardened.

"Mr. Vitello, you're here to fulfill your obligatory community service. I'm here to care for my son," she told him firmly.

Danny didn't even know what to say to that, his eyes widening a degree at her jarring snap. He must've hit a nerve that he hadn't meant to strike.

"Of course … right … I …" he tried to apologize, but she had already spun around and strode down the hallway away from him. He watched her go with a long sigh, his head hanging, visibly deflated.

Despite wanting to sit there and pout over his rough interaction with Maria, Danny knew that he had a job to do, prompting him to head to auditions. Once he got set up in a folding chair on stage in the hospital's auditorium with a clipboard in his hand, he let a few male doctors in to start their auditions for the role of Captain Hook, all of them using a broom handle as a sword.

The first doctor, an old, bald cardiologist, puffed out his chest as he spoke. "Proud and insolent youth … prepare to meet thy doom!"

The second doctor, a younger, slim anesthesiologist, stared down at his script intently. "… to a ten-year-old, I'm huge!"

The third doctor, another older, serious neurologist, nearly stumbled over his simple lines. "I hate, I hate, I hate Peter Pan!"

Danny could only sit there and stare at the doctors as they turned to look at him.

"Well … I guess that was … something. You know the story, right? Peter Pan is Hook's nemesis. Okay … let's try it again with some *emotion!*" Danny stressed, already feeling a sense of dread about this whole production. It was hard enough working with talented cast and crew, but having to work with people outside of the profession was a complete nightmare. He supposed that he deserved the punishment, though. He had messed up, and he kept facing the consequences. He just hadn't realized one of those consequences would come in the form of a play.

Strong sunlight beat down on Brett and Angie's house, sun rays reaching into the living room as Brett ambled through it in a bathrobe with a mug of coffee in his hand. His hair was wet and slicked back from a recent shower, his eyes blinking sleepily. A sudden ping stirred him, drawing his eyes down to Angie's laptop that was on a beautifully crafted wooden desk which sat against one of the living room walls. He moved closer and leaned down to peek at the screen.

Angie's email account was open on the screen, and a new email from "DVitello7777" had just popped up in the notifications. Brett clenched his jaw tightly, an annoyed breath puffing from his nose as he turned his head to gaze out of a nearby window. His eyes landed on Angie laying out by the pool, and he hurriedly read the email.

His eyes skimmed through the beginning and middle before slowing on the last line that read "You're always in my heart, Angie. Love, Danny." With a glare, Brett hastily deleted the email, watching it vanish from her notifications in a flash like it had never existed in the first place.

Back at Cedars-Sinai, Danny strode down the hallway after a half-jogging Linda Schwartz, attempting to catch up to her.

"Um ... hey ... quick question about the play ..." Danny tried to talk to her, his steps quickening as she whipped around the corner.

"I'm on my way to pick up a heart. Join me, Mr. Vitello!" Linda called out to him, not even bothering to pitch a look at him over her shoulder.

An intrigued look filled Danny's face as he followed her, his legs burning from the exertion. He trailed her outside of the hospital to the landing pad, which was painted with a big letter "H."

"It's coming in from Las Vegas. Trauma care is very time sensitive … every minute counts … and here it comes," Linda Schwartz breathed out quickly as she pointed up toward the sky as a low droning sound approached them.

Danny glanced up toward where she was pointing, his eyes landing on a large, red helicopter that was slowly starting to descend. Its rotors kicked up heavy waves of wind that ruffled Danny's dark hair and clothes, the droning of it becoming louder and louder. Pressure soon filled Danny's head, a slipping feeling hitting him as his vision abruptly blacked out.

He wasn't at Cedars-Senai anymore. He was back in Iraq taking cover behind a destroyed building as an Apache helicopter zipped overheard, its rotors rattling noisily. Smoke drifted from bombed buildings, while a golden-domed mosque was in the distance. Insurgents fired at American soldiers from nearby rooftops.

"Elvis, cover me!" Danny cried out before making a run for it as the young soldier unleashed his M-4 to provide cover. He dove into the crook of a bombed building, throwing his arm over his head to cover himself as he heard gunfire all around him. A loud boom sounded, the ground shaking and causing rocks and dust to plummet down on him.

The shaking sensation still stuck with Danny, darkness plaguing his vision until a familiar face came into his sight. He blinked a few times, realizing that Linda was shaking him.

"Are you okay?" Linda cried out, lightly patting his cheek.

Danny's eyes shifted to the side to see the helicopter that had just landed behind her, its loud blades still whirring. He swallowed hard, the sound of his heartbeat pounding heavily in his head. He took a moment to compose himself as much as he could, embarrassment and anxiety clashing within him.

"I'm fine. I just ... blanked out for a second there. I'm good," he answered quietly, tearing his eyes from Linda's.

"Wow. You really did," Linda replied under her breath, continuing to eye him apprehensively.

In Sam's hospital room, Maria hovered over her son, gently pressing a wet compress to Sam's clammy forehead. He looked visibly paler than usual, and his eyes were only halfway open.

"Mom, I'm sorry I'm always sick," he said weakly through his chapped lips.

"Don't you *ever* be sorry! None of this is *your* fault!" Maria told him firmly, her bottom lip trembling slightly as she spoke.

Abruptly, Sam's body started to shake and jerk as he began to seize, his body locking up tightly.

Panic struck Maria as she lunged for the nurse call button, her hands already starting to shake as she watched her son writhe in bed violently.

"Nurse! Help!" Maria called out, looking behind her at the door to Sam's room helplessly. When no one immediately rushed into the room, she darted to the door, not wanting to leave Sam all alone. She glanced up and down the hallway quickly, locating an empty nurse station.

"Please, someone! Help Sam! Help my son! Please, my son needs help!" she screamed down the hallway, her voice echoing off of the white walls.

To her relief, two nurses sprinted down the hallway toward Sam's room with a younger doctor on their heels, their shoes clacking against the tile floor loudly.

Danny stepped out of the elevator in the hallway just as the nurses and the doctor sprinted past him, nearly knocking him over. His eyes trailed them, a confused look gracing his face until it turned into one of shock when he realized that they were running to Sam's room. He rushed after them, nearly crashing into Maria as she stood almost hyperventilating in the doorway. He wrapped his arms around her, holding her close to him as she whimpered and shook, her wide eyes glued to her son as the nurses and the doctor surrounded him.

"Let them do their job. Sam's in good hands," Danny said softly to her, trying to calm her as much as he possibly could. He knew how protective of a mother she was, but he couldn't begin to understand the level of panic that she was feeling right now. He merely squeezed her tighter.

"My boy ... my sweet boy," Maria sobbed in Danny's arms, grabbing at his hands as she nearly slumped in his hold.

Danny brought her closer to his chest, keeping her from collapsing right there. He could feel her shake, her tears plummeting down on his hands and arms. He glanced up to see a young nurse approaching them.

"The doctor is stabilizing him. He'll be fine," the nurse assured them with a comforting smile.

Danny nodded to the nurse, thanking her quietly as his grip on Maria steadily loosened. He glanced down at her, and an awkward moment followed when they realized how close they were to each other.

Maria wiped away her tears and broke apart from Danny, tearing her gaze away from him as she turned to walk over to the nurses and the doctor who were tending to Sam.

Danny watched her go, not missing how rapidly his heart thumped in the depths of his chest.

Chapter Nine

Near silence hung in the hospital's auditorium as Danny leaned back in his chair in front of the stage, his eyes moving to watch a mother and her ten-year-old son walk onstage and stop right in front of him. He straightened up, placing his clipboard in his lap as he looked up to give them a small smile.

"My son, Tommy, would like to recite the Peter Pan monologue," the mother told him as she rubbed her son's back in a comforting manner.

"Okay, whenever he's ready," Danny replied with a nod, giving the boy an encouraging look. He had been in the boy's position before when he was younger and just starting out. He could empathize.

The mother reached forward to try to work the microphone stand down to Tommy's height, but it wouldn't budge.

Danny hopped out of his chair and moved to the edge of the stage to help.

"I'll take care of it," he said as he reached up to lower the stand.

Immediately, vomit spewed out of Tommy's mouth, covering Danny's shirt and arm.

"What the …! Ugh!" Danny cried out, feeling his own stomach churn as he shook his hand to try to fling some of it off of him.

"Sorry," the mother sighed sheepishly before turning to fawn over her son, who was groaning and leaning over.

"Yeah, don't worry about it," Danny grunted as he stepped back from the stage, his body tensing.

"Come on, Tommy. Let's go," the mother told her son, placing her hand on his back to hurry them off of the stage.

Danny gazed down at the vomit dripping down his arms, the very smell making him dizzy. He swallowed hard, beginning to feel off balance as his face warmed up, his forehead growing damp. Shakes trembled over his body as his knees weakened.

"Can somebody get me something to wipe this ..." Danny trailed off, the words coming out slurred as his lips felt numb. Before he could even try to fight it, darkness washed over him.

Danny fell back into Iraq with a deafening boom, his ears ringing as gunfire and explosions sounded all around, sand spraying everywhere. Danny hovered over Corporal Lopez with Elvis at his side, blood staining his arms all the way from his fingertips to his elbows.

Corporal Lopez writhed in pain in the sand, his left leg half torn off from an explosion, the bone showing through tattered skin beneath his pants. His shaky hand grabbed at Danny's arm, yanking him closer.

"Sarge! Get me outta here!" he pleaded, tears streaking down his soot-covered face.

Danny could hardly hear Lopez's anguished cries through all of the battle noise sounding around him, bullets clipping the ground near him in hushed zips.

"Hang on, Lopez! Hang on! Elvis, gimme an IFAK!" Danny shouted, pain searing his throat from shouting so much. Sweat coursed down his face, a few drops burning at his eyes as he gripped Lopez's shoulder, trying to keep him grounded to reality. It wasn't his time to go into the light.

Elvis tossed his satchel on the ground and hurriedly dug through it before yanking out an independent first aid kit. He handed it to Danny, placing his other hand on the back of his head as bullets whizzed past him.

Danny opened the kit and grabbed a huge chunk of gauze to firmly hold down against what remained of Lopez's leg. He looked up to see Lopez's eyes begin to glaze over, his head starting to grow heavy and loll back.

"Stay with me!" Danny shouted at Lopez before another explosion struck the ground nearby, shaking Danny back into the present. He blinked his eyes quickly, looking around at the theater of the hospital. He gritted his teeth, shaking his head to try to coax away any remnants of the memory.

One of the interns from the cast walked up to Danny to offer him a few paper towels.

"Here ya go, Danny," the teenage boy said.

Danny continued to stare straight ahead, his eyes glossing over as he distinctly heard faint explosions in the back of his mind. They were impossible to escape, threatening to blow him to bits at any moment.

"Danny?" the intern said, gazing at Danny in a confused manner.

Danny forced himself back into reality, convincing himself that an explosion wasn't about to end him. He took the paper towels from the intern with a nod before cleaning up the mess the boy had made, though a daze continued to fill his head.

Danny's foot rapidly bounced against the carpeted floor of Dr. Vanowen's office. He knew that he couldn't keep falling out of reality and experiencing those nightmares, so he dragged himself back to Dr. Vanowen to try to figure out a way to put a stop to them.

Dr. Vanowen scribbled on a prescription pad from behind his cluttered desk, his eyes narrowing in concentration.

"In addition to what you're already taking, I'm prescribing something for your nightmares," Dr. Vanowen informed Danny as he ripped a page out of the pad and handed it over to Danny.

Danny reached forward to grab the page, trying his best to steady his hand, but it still shook against his will. He cleared his throat and nodded as he held the page in his hand, its ends crumbling a little in his grip.

"Sometimes they're so bad … I can't go back to sleep," Danny replied, feeling cold all over. He shrunk back into the black and red flannel shirt that he wore over a black T-shirt, trying to find some sort of warmth in the material.

"It's time we start discussing these dreams, Danny … if you're up to it?" Dr. Vanowen said softly, giving Danny an encouraging look.

A faint sigh broke from Danny, his teeth grinding a degree. After having those dreams taint his mind, the last thing that he wanted to do was talk about them, but he knew that he needed to try.

"I guess I gotta be," Danny said.

"Your PTSD has many layers. It's your locked away memories we have to tap into," Dr. Vanowen explained as he rummaged under a few papers to grab a notepad and place it in front of himself, a black pen perched in his hand.

Danny nodded, knowing it would be a rough time, but he just wanted the dreams to go away.

"By the way, did you ever reach out to your ex-wife, Angie?" Dr. Vanowen asked, a curious look crossing his face.

Danny deflated at the mention of Angie, his head shaking slowly.

"No. I mean, I did, but she never … I never heard anything back," Danny explained, still feeling a sting from that. He had put his heart into that email, and she hadn't even bothered to write him back. However, he tried not to let it get to him. He had plenty of other things to worry about.

The next day, Danny decided to visit Sam, figuring it would cheer both him and Sam up. He entered Sam's hospital room, wishing that they would throw a poster up on the wall or at least put a plant in the room. It just looked so bare, almost like a jail cell. His eyes fell on Sam, who was still wired to monitors and had Maria tending to him.

"How's he doing?" Danny asked her as he slowly approached, not wanting to make her angry again.

"He's still running a temperature," Maria sighed as she pitched a quick look over her shoulder at Danny. She turned back around soon after to rest her hand on Sam's forehead to feel the warmth of his skin.

Sam tilted his head to smile at Danny, immediately seeming to perk up at the sight of him.

"Hey, champ," Danny greeted him warmly as he stopped next to Maria at Sam's bedside.

"I'll let you guys visit," Maria said before turning away to head out of the room.

"How's the play going?" Sam asked Danny, his face still harboring a hint of a pale tone. However, to Danny's delight, he looked much better than he did the other day.

Danny shrugged, not bothering to mention the whole vomit situation that had happened yesterday.

"Haven't got anyone for the role of Peter Pan yet. You wouldn't be interested, would ya?" Danny asked him, lifting his eyebrows. Sam was a passionate and driven kid. He had the spirit that Danny needed.

An unsure look crossed Sam's face.

"Me? I don't know. I've never acted before. I'm not really ..." Sam started to make up excuses until Danny cut him off.

"But you know acting. You've watched tons of movies. You remember lines. You sure remembered mine, right?" Danny pointed out with a small smile. The kid was more apt for acting than he gave himself credit for.

Sam glanced down at his hands, looking embarrassed.

"Once, I had to give a report in front of my class. I was so nervous that I almost peed my pants," Sam explained.

"You know what my first role *ever* was?" Danny asked Sam.

Sam shook his head, an intrigued look coming onto his face.

"Peter Pan. I was in fourth grade," Danny replied with a soft laugh as a look of disbelief overtook Sam's expression. It was a complete coincidence, but *Peter Pan* was his favorite for multiple reasons.

"Nuh uh. You're making that up!" Sam said with a shake of his head.

Danny held up three fingers, a serious expression crossing his face.

"Scout's honor! Everyone knows that the role of Peter Pan is the role of a lifetime," Danny pointed out, having enjoyed playing Peter Pan when he was younger. It was a spirited, exciting role to play. He reached into the back pocket of his jeans to pull out a folded *Peter Pan* script, flipping through the pages.

"There's a line in here … oh, here it is. 'The moment you doubt you can fly, you cease for ever to be able to do it,'" Danny read the line before looking up past the pages at Sam.

Sam seemed to ponder on the words, looking intrigued.

"So … like, if you don't think you can do something, then you won't ever be able to do it?" Sam asked for clarification.

"Exactly! Remember the boy who played my son in *The Road Block*?" Danny asked him, lifting an eyebrow.

"Sure do. Little John!" Sam quipped as he straightened up in bed.

Danny nodded with a bright smile.

"Well, we used to rehearse lines together every day," Danny explained, remembering those times. He had been nervous at first to work with a child actor, but they were far more practiced and disciplined than he gave them credit for.

"Would you rehearse lines with me, too?" Sam asked him, a hopeful look shining in his wide eyes.

"Of course!" Danny agreed, waving the script in front of Sam enticingly.

An excited laugh broke from Sam as he grabbed the script from Danny and started flipping through the pages, his eyes alight with the spirit that Danny was searching for.

Gelson's Market was bustling with shoppers as they moved from aisle to aisle to pick up the finest produce and freshest meats, their carts rolling over sleek tile flooring. Brett and Angie halted near the butcher's department so that Brett could take a quick selfie with a young female fan. Angie watched from the side, waiting patiently for Brett to turn away from the fan. Once the girl had gone, Brett picked up a good-sized turkey and presented it to Angie for her approval.

"That's *way* too big, Mr. Casanova," Angie smirked at him as she crossed her arms over her red tank top.

Brett laughed as he shrugged.

"Gotta keep the fans happy," he replied.

Angie smiled and shook her head at him, her eyes trailing to the side and landing on Markus with Lydia. She watched them push a cart near the fruits and vegetables department that bordered the butcher's department.

"Hon, I'm going to say a quick hello to Markus and Lydia. Be right back," Angie told him.

Brett looked over their way, but he didn't wave or nod to them.

"Okay, babe," he said before turning to look back at some of the meat cuts.

Angie hurried toward the fruits and vegetables department to catch up to Markus and Lydia, who turned and immediately hugged her once they saw her.

"Here's our girl!" Markus exclaimed as he rubbed her upper back warmly.

"We miss you," Lydia nearly pouted the words as she smiled at Angie.

"I really miss you guys, too!" Angie replied, beaming brightly until it started to diminish under a more serious look. She glanced back at Brett before turning back toward Markus and Lydia.

"I should have called you. How is he?" Angie asked them quietly.

Markus and Lydia shared a brief look.

"You know, Danny's … a strong guy, but he's struggling. He's still fightin' that damn war," Markus sighed with a shake of his head.

"We're loving on him as best we can. He's been at Cedars …" Lydia started to explain until Angie gasped.

"Cedars? What happened?" Angie asked, a worried expression exploding on her face as she looked between the two of them.

"Oh, no. He's fine. He's putting together a Christmas show for the kids," Markus explained.

Angie sighed with relief, drawing her fingers through her hair to pull back a few strands that had fallen into her face.

"Danny and his big heart," Angie replied, her eyes seeming to haze over as she sank back into her thoughts and memories. Soon, tears started to collect in her eyes, and she tried to blink them away.

"I'm so thankful that he has you two," Angie gulped, sounding choked up.

"He's the little brother I never had," Markus chuckled warmly.

Angie merely smiled and nodded, her throat swelling too much for her to say anything. She gave Lydia a grateful look as Lydia reached forward to wipe a tear off of Angie's face.

"I better go," Angie finally sighed out, knowing that Brett was waiting for her.

"You take care of yourself, Angie," Markus told her gently before he and Lydia moved forward to embrace her.

Angie imparted a faint goodbye before heading back to Brett, sniffling quietly and dabbing at her eyes before she reached him.

Brett held up a frozen turkey as he stood in front of a freezer section.

"How's this one?" Brett asked her.

Angie felt her eyes burn again, making them shine over. Thankfully, Brett didn't notice.

"It's fine," Angie replied quietly, not even caring about the turkey anymore.

"They mention anything about Danny?" Brett asked, cocking an eyebrow at her.

Angie snapped out of her thoughts to look at him, a flush of anxiety rushing through her.

"What? Um, yeah ... he's putting together a show at Cedars," she explained to him, already regretting saying anything when an amused smirk quirked up on his face. She tried not to talk to Brett about Danny if she could avoid the topic.

"Your ex's career really is in 'critical condition,' huh?" Brett laughed out.

Angie rolled her eyes at him, not finding his joke very funny at all. His sense of humor grated against her at times, but she usually tried to look past it.

"Don't be a jerk, Brett!" she snapped at him, swatting at his arm only to catch his blue T-shirt sleeve.

"I'm kidding, babe," Brett smirked at her before patting her backside.

Angie glared at him, her jaw clenching.

"And *don't* slap my ass either!" she growled, not appreciating the motion, especially since she was already upset. He knew not to mess with her when she was like this.

"Come on! I said I was kidding," Brett sighed as he placed a hand on her back to draw her close to him. He placed a soft kiss on her forehead, his hand rubbing gentle circles on her lower back.

Angie found herself melting into the touch, her head tilting up to give him a forgiving look. It was hard to stay mad sometimes.

On Thanksgiving night, Danny strode into Sam's room with a large shopping bag in his hand. He found Sam asleep and Maria sitting on the edge of Sam's bed, her eyes on the television as an old movie played. Danny quieted his movements as he approached Sam's bedside.

"Happy Thanksgiving!" he whisper-shouted to Maria, who cracked a smile at him.

"Hi. Happy Thanksgiving!" Maria whispered back to him.

Sam stirred, his eyes blinking open slowly as a yawn broke from him.

"Hi, Danny," Sam mumbled sleepily once he noticed that Danny was in the room.

"Look who's up," Maria mused as she turned to smile at Sam. She reached forward to gently take his hand, giving it a warm squeeze.

"Hey, Champ, lookin' good. I brought food," Danny quipped as he held up the large shopping bag. There had been plenty of leftovers after he had Thanksgiving dinner with Markus and Lydia, and they made sure there was plenty to bring to Sam and Maria. He figured that the hospital wouldn't throw him a Thanksgiving dinner, so Danny was going to do it himself.

"Yes! I'm starving!" Sam groaned out as he slowly pushed himself into a sitting position, being mindful of his monitors and wires.

Maria watched Danny and Sam quietly, a warm smile crossing her lips uncontrollably as she sat off to the side.

Danny glanced over to see Maria watching him mess around with Sam, and a friendly smile was shared between them. He felt something flutter in his chest in response, but he pushed away the feeling so that he could focus on getting Sam fixed up for the holiday. He set the shopping bag on Sam's bed and pulled out red Tupperware bowls full of turkey and mashed potatoes. He laid out paper plates and cups on the small hospital table cart that rested in the far corner of the room, fixing it up nicely for Sam.

"I'll have a plate set up for you in a jiffy, Sam," Danny told him warmly as he started fixing Sam a plate, his eyes shifting over to Maria every once in a while to see her smiling. He must've been doing something right for her to be looking at him like that, prompting him to smile to himself and kick off their Thanksgiving dinner.

Auditions for the play continued in full swing after the holiday ended. Danny sat near the front of the stage in a pair of black joggers, a white T-shirt, and a red baseball cap, while a group of parents and their kids watched other children rehearse on stage from the seats.

"Who's next?" Danny called out from his chair, the tip of his pen clicking against his clipboard.

A father lifted his hand to Danny as he wheeled his nine-year-old daughter across the stage in her wheelchair. He patted his daughter on the shoulder encouragingly before moving back over to the side to stand with his wife.

"And what's your name?" Danny asked the young girl, giving her a warm smile. He could tell that she was nervous, but he wanted her to have a good time, too.

The girl glanced down at her feet anxiously, avoiding Danny's eyes as her blonde hair fell into her face.

"You can do it, Janie," her father called to her from side stage.

Janie lifted her head slowly, gazing out at the audience with wide eyes, looking frozen.

Danny heard a few kids in the audience snicker quietly, making him clench his jaw a degree to keep himself from whipping around and yelling at them to shut up. He watched the mother and father share frowns as their daughter had a tough time on stage. He stood from his chair and moved over to her, squatting down to her level.

"Hi, Janie. I'm Danny," he said gently, his eyes sweeping over her green T-shirt and white leggings. He had a feeling about who she was auditioning for.

Janie's parents watched Danny lean forward to whisper something to Janie before chatting with her, making Janie smile and laugh, the sound echoing throughout the auditorium.

Danny shot Janie an encouraging smile before walking back over to his chair to sit down.

"Okay, sweetheart, whenever you're ready," he told her with a nod, knowing that she could do it. She had spirit.

With all of the confidence of a seasoned actor, Janie lifted her chin and spoke, projecting her voice out to the audience.

"All you need is faith, trust, and a little bit of pixie dust!" Janie recited her line with confidence and a glowing smile. She looked over at Danny, who shot her a wink and a smile. Her mouth dropped open in shock as people in the auditorium applauded her.

Her parents gazed at each other excitedly as they clapped and cheered for their daughter.

The hospital administrator, Mrs. Schwartz, watched contently from the back of the room, a small smile crossing her lips as she admired the scene.

Danny folded his arms and smiled proudly, enjoyment flooding through him. Maybe putting on this play wouldn't be as bad as he originally thought it would be. He needed to find his spirit, too, and it was coming back in small traces. He was just grateful that it was coming back at all.

Chapter Ten

The next day, Danny walked into the entrance of the hospital's lobby, nodding politely to the receptionist. His eyes ventured to the right, making him stop in his tracks as his eyes fell on Angie. Actually, she was on the television playing in the waiting area. It was on mute, but Danny could tell that it was a shampoo commercial.

Danny watched her talk to the camera with a shampoo bottle in her hand. She tossed her hair back with a bright smile, coaxing one of Danny's own onto his face as he admired her performance. He pulled out his phone and texted a quick message before continuing on his way.

Across town, at Brett and Angie's house, Angie stood in the kitchen with sweat adorning her forehead and her body clad in a sports bra and yoga pants. She blended a green smoothie, hearing her phone ding. Turning her head, she glanced at the text that had just popped up on her phone screen.

Hey Ang, never heard back from my email. I totally understand, just wanted to say congrats on the shampoo spot! I always said you had great hair! :)

With a confused frown, Angie abandoned her smoothie to head to the living room, moving to sit at her desk in front of her laptop. She opened it and started clicking around, accessing her recently deleted mail. She scrolled down, her eyes widening as she spotted Danny's email address.

"Deleted?" she whispered to herself, not remembering deleting an email from Danny. She didn't even remember receiving an email from Danny. She immediately opened the email, leaning forward to read through the message.

Angie, Hope this finds you happy and well. I want to tell you that I'm sorry. When I look back at the time we shared, I'm not sure why you stuck with me as long as you did. I'm finally taking your advice and getting help. I'm not sure if it will do any good or if they can fix me, but I'm gonna try. Thanks for being in my corner and bailing me out of jail, too:) You're always in my heart, Angie.

Love,

Danny

Angie didn't realize that she was crying until she felt a tear roll down her cheek, her hand lifting to wipe it away with a soft sniffle.

"Hey," Brett's voice surprisingly sounded from behind her.

A frightened gasp jumped from Angie as she spun around in her office chair, her heart hammering against her chest as she saw Brett in the kitchen. For a second, she had thought that he was right behind her. Thankfully, he was in an entirely different room, too far for him to see her laptop screen.

"Woah! Didn't mean to startle you," Brett chuckled as he adjusted the collar of his yellow Polo shirt, his other hand moving to drop his wallet and car keys down on the kitchen counter.

"Oh, no, just answering some ... fan mail," Angie stammered, putting her body in front of her laptop screen to ensure that he couldn't see anything. She swallowed hard, afraid that he'd somehow be able to hear her loud heartbeat.

Brett nodded as he turned toward the blender on the granite counter, an interested look crossing his face as he leaned close to peer into the blender container.

"Mind if I finish your smoothie?" he asked her, pointing to the green concoction that she had abandoned.

"No, go ahead," Angie replied with a nod, her body still remaining tense. She prompted herself to spin back around and quickly exit out of her deleted emails once Brett disappeared off into the house with his smoothie. She looked at her phone, feeling a pulling sensation on her mind. She grabbed her phone and texted Danny back, a small smile teasing at her lips as her fingers flew over the keyboard.

You just made my day!

Angie stared at the text message, a thought coming to her mind that she tried to fight but failed to. She added *XOXO* to the end of the text, her forefinger hitting the send button before she could chicken out and change her mind.

Back at Cedars-Sinai, as Danny headed away from the lobby to venture down the hallway, his phone dinged. He reached into his pocket and pulled his phone out to read Angie's new message, a smile crossing his face as his heart jolted. He hadn't expected a text back, but he couldn't begin to describe how happy it made him to receive one anyway.

Later that day, Danny headed into Sam's room for a visit, his eyes falling onto the television, which was playing the movie *Hook*. Pride flushed through Danny as he crossed his arms and glanced over at Sam, who was sitting up straight in his bed with an intrigued look on his face.

"You took my advice! How ya likin' the movie?" Danny asked him as he moved to stand at Sam's bedside, smiling a little at how messy and scattered Sam's dark hair looked.

Sam didn't have a care in the world, though. He was too focused on the movie, his mouth twisting into a slight frown.

"It's great, but isn't he too old to be Peter Pan?" Sam asked as he turned his head to look at Danny, a few strands of hair falling against his forehead. He seemed to be swallowed up by the white hospital gown he wore, the material not fitting quite right.

Danny wished that Sam could at least be able to wear normal kid clothes or be able to go outside of the hospital for an hour or two. He was so confined here, but Danny figured it was worth it for Sam to get better.

"I guess, but the Lost Boys see him as a kid, just like them. Great acting, though, huh?" Danny asked him, having always loved this movie and its cast. So many different movies and actors had inspired him starting out, and he hoped that Sam had gotten some inspiration for the play while watching this movie.

"How come Robin Williams committed suicide?" Sam asked, taking the conversation down a completely different path than Danny expected.

Danny nearly flinched at the question, his eyes blinking a few times in shock at the sudden question. He didn't expect to talk about such a subject with a kid.

"You know about that?" Danny questioned, wondering how Sam knew about that and what all did he know about what had happened.

"Before the movie started, they were talking about it. Wasn't he rich?" Sam asked, looking completely confused.

Danny lifted his hand to scratch at the back of his neck awkwardly, trying to figure out how to approach the subject in an appropriate manner for a child. It was tough enough talking about it with adults.

"Well, yeah, but rich people still get sad, and sometimes it's too much, even if you're famous," Danny explained, his words coming out slowly. He wasn't sure if Sam would understand that, but that was the most kid-friendly explanation that he could think of.

"I don't get why anyone would *want* to die?" Sam speculated with a small shake of his head, a frown remaining on his face.

Danny could understand why Sam thought that. He was in a bad position himself with his health, having been on the verge of death. He was a child. The last thing that he wanted was to die, and Danny could only hope that Sam maintained that mentality as he got older.

"It's like a ... bad disease ... that just takes over your mind," Danny replied.

"That really stinks," Sam stated with a nod, understanding what that was like in his own way.

"Yeah ... it does," Danny agreed, having found himself in dark places before. They were hard to escape as they continued to haunt him in various forms, whether they were nightmares or something else going wrong in his life due to his past choices.

Sam tilted his head up to look at Danny, a curious look appearing on his face once again as his mind wandered.

"Danny, do you have a girlfriend?"

A confused look crossed Danny's face, being blindsided by another random topic to figure out how to talk about with a kid.

"Uh … not at the moment. Why?" Danny questioned Sam, wondering where this was all coming from.

Sam sighed and shrugged his shoulders.

"I wish you were my mom's boyfriend. If I die, I want to know that she has someone who makes her happy," Sam said quietly.

Danny stared at Sam in complete shock, not understanding why he was thinking such things. He was so young and innocent. He shouldn't be worrying about things like that. He just needed to focus on getting better.

"Sam … you … you're not … why would you even think you're gonna die?" Danny asked, wondering if something had happened that no one told him about or if Sam was just overthinking things.

Sam stared into his lap at his hands, his fingers threading together in an uneasy manner.

"I've known other kids who died. They were here, sick like me, and then a few months later … they weren't," Sam replied in a quiet voice, his eyes lifting to glance around the room, like he expected to see the lost children there near him.

Danny moved closer to Sam's bedside, giving him a comforting look.

"A lot of kids get better. *You're* gonna get better," Danny told him firmly, believing his own words with every fiber of his being. Sam had to get better. He just had to.

Sam nodded, a small smile crossing his lips. He seemed a bit more at ease.

"I just wish she had someone nice, like you. She deserves it," Sam said, a wistful look in his dark eyes.

Danny didn't say anything, not even knowing what he could say to that. Maria did deserve someone nice, but he wasn't sure if he was good enough for her. He had been caught up in a lot of trouble, and he was still trying to dig himself out of the hole. He didn't want to drag Maria or Sam down into it with him. He reached out to rub Sam's head, smiling warmly at him instead.

The next day, Danny spent some time with Markus and Lydia, using the time to relax for a little while after all of the hard work and energy that he had been spending on the play. Things were coming together nicely. There were a few bumps in the road here and there, but that was showbiz.

"Come on! Run it!" Markus shouted at the television as he and Danny watched a game of college football.

Lydia entered the living room with a few items in her hands. She gave them to Danny with a beaming smile.

"Here you go, Mister Director. Moccasins, size four, and Tinkerbell wings, as requested," she quipped in a proud manner, tilting her head up.

Danny gazed down at the handcrafted shoes and wings, a look of awe crossing his face. Lydia was a miracle worker and such a saving grace for his production.

"Lydia, you're amazing! These wings are perfect! You're going to make one little girl very happy. Thank you!" Danny told her sincerely, already able to imagine the smile in response to these costume pieces. He had wanted to do something special for Janie, and he hoped that this would make her smile.

"Well, you let her know that it was my pleasure," Lydia replied as she patted Danny's shoulder.

"You're one lucky man, Markus," Danny announced as he turned to smile at his friend. Markus and Lydia were a perfect match, one that Danny found himself envious of at times. They were made for each other, and it would destroy Danny if anything ever happened to them.

"Don't I know it. She keeps me grinnin' like a possum eatin' a sweet tater," Markus chuckled as he held a hand out to Lydia, drawing her close to him.

Lydia smiled warmly and leaned down to press a kiss to the top of his head lovingly.

Danny watched them with a smile, hoping that he would have a bond like that with someone. He missed being held and holding someone. Loneliness struck him hard when he least expected it, but he just tried to look past it and move forward. He had work to do.

The auditorium's stage was full of cast members as rehearsal took place, chattering and thumping sounding all around as people moved across the stage and practiced their lines. It was chaotic, but everyone seemed to be having fun taking a break from reality to invest in a short period of fantasy. They could be whoever they wanted to be. They didn't have to be a doctor working to save someone's life or a sick patient. They could be Peter Pan or a Lost Boy or a fairy. The limits were boundless.

"Danny, are you sure that I'll be able to do the show while in my chair?" Janie asked as she gazed up at him, a worried look gracing her face.

"Absolutely! There's a lot of fairies that have to get around like that," Danny told her with a smile, like it was a well-known fact. He didn't want her to worry and stress out. This was all supposed to be fun, and she would make a great Tinkerbell.

"I told ya," Sam voiced from next to Janie, shooting her a toothy grin. He was ecstatic about being out of his hospital bed and being able to move about and talk to people. It was lonely being kept in that hospital room of his.

"Oh, good! And, Danny, am I really going to be your official date for the play, like you said?" Janie asked, a shy smile crossing her face as she blushed.

Danny placed his hand over his chest and nodded, swearing to her.

"A gentleman doesn't go back on his word. I mean, if it's okay with Sam," Danny replied as he turned his head to smile at Sam.

Sam smiled back and nodded.

"Just this once," Sam replied in a warning tone, giving Danny a playful look.

Janie extended her arms out for a hug, looking overwhelmed with happiness, her eyes even sparkling a degree.

Danny leaned down to hug her gently, patting her back as he felt her press a quick kiss to his cheek. Warmth accumulated in his face as he pulled away and smiled at her, knowing that she had been acting so much happier and brighter since her audition. He had sympathy for her and everything that she had to go through, and he just wanted to make her happy, to show her that she could still have fun and exciting moments in her life, no matter what. He would show her that it was worth it, even if things were dark at times.

While everyone else was at rehearsal, Maria and Dr. Kumar spoke together in Sam's room. Dr. Kumar held Sam's chart in his hands as he examined it, humming to himself before looking up at Maria.

"I can arrange for Sam to be home for Christmas, but I need to do another spinal tap to check his CS fluid," Dr. Kumar explained to her as he tucked the chart beneath his arm.

Maria sighed as she shook her head, a look of dismay filling her face.

"He dreads that more than anything. Maybe knowing that he can go home afterwards, though ..." she trailed off, hoping for the best.

"I have an opening Friday at noon," Dr. Kumar told her with a sympathetic smile.

Maria nodded after a moment.

"Okay, thank you, Doctor. I can't tell you how wonderful it will be to have my sweet boy back home finally," Maria said, giving Dr. Kumar a grateful look.

Dr. Kumar reached out to pat her arm warmly before walking out of the room, passing Danny and Sam as they headed inside of Sam's room.

"Sam, your mom has some news for you," Dr. Kumar commented, shooting Sam a wink before heading down the hallway.

Danny paused at the doorway as Sam walked inside to join his mother, who had a bright look on her face. He guessed that it was personal news, and he didn't want to be in the way.

"I'll give you guys some privacy," he voiced as he started to back away to give Sam and Maria some time to talk.

Maria waved her hand, gesturing for him to come inside as she moved to sit on the edge of Sam's bed.

"No, please stay," she replied.

Sam smiled at that, receiving a quick wink from Danny. He hopped up on the bed next to Maria, leaning close with a curious look on his face.

"What kind of news, Mom?" he asked, looking a bit nervous.

"The doctor said pack your bags, little man. You're going home!" Maria announced to him, smiling joyfully.

"Really? That's awesome!" Sam gasped out as he bounced a little on the spot.

Danny could've bounced with him, but he noticed that Maria's smile faltered a little. There was something else. He stayed quiet, feeling a current of nervousness run through him as he waited to hear the other part of the news.

"One thing, though …" Maria added, nearly wincing at her own words as she lowered her eyes to her lap.

Sam stopped moving, his eyes narrowing a little as he eyed her closely.

"Not the needle?" Sam asked quietly, a frown crossing his face as his eyes widened in realization.

Maria turned to him as she grabbed his hand, a guilty look crossing her face.

"I know you don't like it, but we'll be able to get you home," she reasoned with him.

Sam dropped his head, burying his face in his hands as he groaned.

Danny narrowed his eyes in confusion, wondering what they were talking about. It obviously wasn't something good, judging from Sam's devastated reaction and Maria's guilty one. It saddened him that Sam had been so happy one moment and then distraught the next.

"What needle?" Danny asked.

Sam shot his head up to look at Danny with an anxious expression.

"This huge needle that they put in my back! I hate it!" he nearly cried out, shaking his head.

Danny nodded in understanding, realizing what Sam was talking about. He had never had the procedure done, but he was pretty sure that he had seen it on television or something to that extent. It looked like a painful and uncomfortable procedure, one that he wished Sam didn't have to go through, but Danny knew that it was necessary. An idea came to his mind, but he was cautious with saying it, knowing that it likely wasn't his place. However, he wanted to comfort Sam as much as he possibly could.

"Well, if the doctor lets me, and your mom thinks it's okay, maybe I could be there with you?" Danny offered with a hopeful look. If he was going through a scary procedure, he would want people to be there for him. However, he didn't want to cross any boundaries with Maria.

"Really? I won't be scared if you're there," Sam replied with a hint of a smile breaking out across his face. He turned to give Maria a pleading look, complete with puppy dog eyes.

Maria looked at Sam, a smile crossing her lips at his expression. She turned to Danny with a nod and a grateful look.

"That would be really great, Danny," she told him sincerely, a soft look adorning her face now as she gazed at him.

Danny felt his heart flutter a bit at Maria's genuinely grateful look. He coaxed himself past the feeling, needing to focus on making sure that Sam was game for his procedure.

"I'm there!" Danny promised.

"Thanks, Danny!" Sam exclaimed cheerfully as he hopped off of the bed and ran into Danny's arms, gripping him around the waist in a firm embrace.

"It's this Friday at noon," Maria commented to Danny as she watched the two hug, her eyes seeming to glow at the sight.

Danny patted Sam's back before releasing him.

"Perfect. I already canceled rehearsals for Friday because I have a meeting to go to," Danny replied with a nod. Sam's procedure lined up perfectly with his schedule. He would've canceled anything to make sure that he was with Sam, though. That was something that he would never miss out on.

"Danny's got an important meeting with some agents," Sam quipped, flashing Danny a proud smile.

"Oh, really?" Maria asked within a small laugh, her eyebrows lifting as she looked over at Danny.

Danny shrugged, trying to be lowkey about it. He didn't want to jinx anything, but Sam was firm on the fact that this could be Danny's next break. Danny appreciated the support. He sure did need it.

"Yeah, if I can get in with them, I got a good shot at making movies again," Danny explained, hoping that everything would pan out. Directing the play made him miss acting a lot, so he hoped that this could be his way back in.

"We're pulling for you, Danny," Maria told him warmly, giving him an encouraging nod.

Gratitude flooded Danny as he smiled at her, knowing that she meant it. Most of the tension between them had gone away, but he was still mindful around her. He wanted to stay on her good side, to get to know her more. She was still a mystery to him, and he was interested in knowing more about her outside of being Sam's mother.

"I know ya are. And afterwards, to celebrate you getting out of here, how about I take you guys on a VIP studio lot tour? I still got a *few* connections," Danny suggested, having not burned all of his bridges just yet. He had a few still standing that he could use, and he wanted to treat them with a nice day outside of the hospital.

Sam audibly gasped, his jaw dropping in shock.

"Yes! That'll be so awesome!" Sam cheered.

"That is so sweet of you!" Maria told Danny sincerely, flashing a smile at Sam, who threw himself back into Danny's arms for a second hug.

Danny chuckled and held Sam close, his head lifting to share a smile with Maria. He couldn't help but feel attached to them both. They had grown on him, becoming a part of his day, a constant thought in his mind. He hoped dearly that he wouldn't lose them.

Later that day, Danny headed toward the auditorium stage door, his ears catching onto a faint sound that grew stronger and stronger the closer that he got. He realized that it was the sound of a piano being played quite masterfully, the notes rolling smoothly after each other. Unable to help his curiosity, Danny opened the door slightly and peeked his head inside.

On stage, Janie drifted her fingers along the keys of the piano, playing a beautiful melody as her parents watched with pride off to the side.

Danny's jaw nearly dropped as he watched, feeling completely mesmerized by her talent. He had no idea the little shy girl had this gift. He felt his mind start to slip, drawing him back into a past memory of his own.

A younger version of himself sat on a piano bench with his little brother and their mother sitting between them. She played the piano with ease and sang softly to them.

"… and the two little boys played with their toys and made all kinds of …" she trailed off to let them finish the line with a smile.

"Noise!" Danny and his brother shouted, sparking laughter between them as their mother wrapped her arms around them, drawing them close and kissing their heads lovingly.

Danny shot back to the present, a warm feeling filling his chest as he thought back on the memory. Those had been good times, ones full of warmth and love. He missed them dearly, able to feel them in small moments such as these. He continued to watch Janie play, a twinkle and a tear sparkling in his eyes.

Chapter Eleven

On Friday, Danny, dressed to the nines in a recently dry-cleaned, well-fitted suit, stared up at a tall and magnificent building with the insignia of the United Artists Agency on it in large gold letters. He swallowed down his nervousness, knowing that this was something that he needed to do with full confidence. He couldn't walk in there with his tail between his legs. He had to be bold and be brave.

He walked inside and started hanging out in the waiting area for a while. Danny cracked his knuckles quietly as he sat up straight on a plush couch in the modernly designed room. Everything looked sharp and clean, almost making him feel like he shouldn't touch anything, from the glistening tile floor to the marble coffee table in front of him.

Dianna, an older, stylish agent, entered the waiting area from a nearby room. She strode over to Danny and shook his hand energetically, her short cut, brown hair bouncing with each movement.

"Danny! Welcome! Please come in," she greeted him as she led him through a door into a conference room with big windows along one wall.

Danny glanced around the room to see six other agents in suits and blazers seated around a large table in the middle, eyeing him intently. Once Dianna took her seat at the head of the table, Danny moved to sit down in a free seat, clearing his throat quietly as he smoothed his suit down. He tried not to let all of the eyes on him get to him, but they were fairly hard to ignore.

"Thanks for coming in, Danny. We're all fans of your work," Dianna voiced with a bright smile.

"I appreciate you giving me a meeting. I'm definitely ready to get back out there," Danny replied, giving them all a grateful look. He could've kissed their feet at that point because he was so desperate for a mere chance.

"Tell us what you've been working on, Danny," Dianna invited him to elaborate.

Danny nodded, sitting up straight as he clasped his hands in front of him.

"I mean, as far as feature acting goes, it's been a while since I've worked. My last couple projects had some hiccups," Danny explained, trying to remain calm as he was greeted with stares. He knew that "hiccups" was a mild explanation for everything that had actually gone down, but he really needed these people to like him. He didn't need to air out all of his dirty laundry. He was sure that they already knew anyway.

"But I've been directing ..." Danny started back up again until Dianna cut into his sentence.

"A feature? Television show?" Dianna inquired, leaning forward a bit as she gave him a curious look.

Danny laughed softly, shifting uncomfortably in his chair. He wished that he could be directing something like that, but he had to start from the very bottom and work his way up.

"Actually, it's a children's theater at Cedars-Sinai hospital," Danny explained, his eyes shifting to watch one of the male agents nudge and snicker to a female agent. He felt coldness flush over him as his anxiety ramped back up. He didn't think it was something to laugh about, but all of these people thought that they were better than he was to begin with.

"It's a community service thing …" Danny commented, but he didn't think that anything that he said even mattered. He scanned their faces, noting their smirks, or their lack of attention in general, as they stared down at their iPads, phones, and laptops. He felt invisible at that point, and he felt like his shot had already been lost.

Danny trudged down the hallway of the hospital in the same suit that he wore to the meeting, his shoulders sagging. Those agents weren't interested in him. They hardly even looked his way. He tried to push the disappointment out of his mind, but it trailed him like a shadow. He carried the Tinkerbell wings in his hand as he walked, figuring a visit to Janie would put him in better spirits. He passed by a young nurse, who whipped around to look at him.

"Danny! Nurse Sally was looking for you," she told him before he continued down the hallway.

Danny nodded, thanking her quietly. He would get to Nurse Sally later. Right now, he wanted to see Janie, whose room was just up ahead. He pushed the door open a little and peered inside, his eyes landing on a young boy in the bed with his parents nearby instead. He narrowed his eyes in confusion, stumbling over a hushed apology as he backed away from the room, guessing that he got the room number wrong.

"Danny!"

Danny turned upon hearing his name being called from down the hallway. He spotted Nurse Sally striding across the white tile his way.

116

"Hey! I wasn't sure if we'd see you today," Nurse Sally commented as she stopped in front of him, placing her hands on her hips.

Danny shrugged with a faint smile as he lifted the Tinkerbell wings up.

"I was gonna drop these off to Janie. Did they move her or something?" he asked as he nodded to the room with the boy in it.

Nurse Sally's face slowly dropped as she stared at Danny, a confused look filling her face.

"Oh … I thought you heard … she's not with us anymore, Danny," she told him softly as she shook her head.

Danny narrowed his eyes in confusion, not understanding what she meant. He figured that someone would've told him if Janie had been moved to a new hospital or floor.

"Wait, what? Where'd she go?" Danny asked her.

A look of anguish flooded Nurse Sally's face, her hand reaching out to his shoulder.

A feeling of realization struck Danny, his chest tightening as his head shook.

"No …" he breathed out, his throat swelling so tightly that it pained him. She had just been here. He had just seen her, promising her everything. She couldn't be gone just like that. He hadn't kept his word to her.

"Danny," Nurse Sally sighed, trying to pull him close, but Danny yanked himself away.

The floor beneath him felt like it was tilting, the walls growing closer. Danny had to get out of the hospital; he felt like it was threatening to swallow him whole. He stumbled down the hallway, not even knowing where his steps were taking him. He tore at the top few buttons of his button-down, unable to properly breathe, but even that release of pressure didn't help him. He left the hospital and just kept walking and walking until the sun collapsed into darkness, and he found himself staring at the train tracks of the LA Metro Red Line Subway System.

Danny slowly focused in on reality, but he still felt like he was outside of his own body. He knew that he was holding the Tinkerbell wings in his hand, but he couldn't feel them against his fingertips. He knew that people were all around him waiting for their trains and that announcements were playing over the subway's speaker system, but his head was full of white noise.

She was really gone.

"Next stop, Hollywood Vine Station," a muffled announcement sounded in the background.

Danny blinked a few times as he stood right on the edge of the platform, wishing that the darkness inside of the tunnel would just snatch him up. He didn't feel any light around him. A strong breeze swept from the tunnel and quickly knocked the Tinkerbell wings from his hand. He watched them float away from him as a train approached from the other side, its wheels screeching louder and louder. The sound filled his ears, bleeding into the white noise and knocking him away from reality.

The screeching noise turned into loud machine gun fire, the rapid popping sounding all around Danny as he ran through the warzone of Iraq. The body armor that he had above his combat fatigues wore down on his muscles as he clutched his M-4 rifle to his chest. His boots thumped heavily against the ground, smoke and dust wisping around him as he dodged gunfire. Sweat stung at his eyes, but he kept them focused on a burnt-out car up ahead.

"IED! IED!" Danny shouted, pain searing through his throat.

At that moment, a heavy blast erupted in front of him, solid white slamming Danny backwards into pure darkness.

"Hey, fella, you alright?" an old man's voice shouted through the darkness.

Danny snapped back into the present, his brain lagging behind. He was kneeling on the platform next to the tracks, a group of people staring at him. He tilted his head up toward the direction of the voice, his vision blurring a degree. It looked like another soldier was standing above him. He blinked a few times, the blur fading into sharpness as he made out an older man instead.

He had slipped once again. Danny moved away from the crowd silently, leaning against the railing of the stairs as he hauled himself up them. Wherever he went, pain chased him down. Once he made it to the sidewalk outside, his knees threatened to buckle, forcing him to sit down against a wall as the sun beamed down on him. He groaned and pulled his jacket over his head, blocking out his surroundings to try to find a moment of peace within his own mind.

Through the jacket, Danny could make out shadows drifting by him. He rummaged through his pocket to grab his phone, lowering his head to see that he had a missed call and a voicemail. He pressed the phone to his ear, his heart sinking into his chest as Sam's voice came on over the speaker.

"Hi, Danny. Just wondering where you are. You weren't at my procedure, and we're late for the Studio Lot Tour. Hope you're okay."

Danny dropped his phone into his lap as his body wilted, his eyes welling with tears as he curled into the darkness of his jacket's cover.

It took until dusk for Danny to gather himself, but when he finally did, he made his way to Maria's house, knowing that he had a lot of apologizing and groveling to do. After hearing about Janie passing, he had just lost himself, letting himself drift away into the wind. He knew that was a problem, one that he needed to get a grip on soon. He couldn't keep losing track of his time and his life.

Danny spotted Sam playing in the front yard of the house by himself, tossing a baseball in the air and then catching it with his glove. The house was brick with a black-shingled roof and a wooden porch adorned with potted plants and a doormat. He wondered how long it had been since Sam had been back home. He approached Sam from behind, putting a small smile on his face. It was nice to see Sam in normal clothes of a green T-shirt and black athletic shorts instead of a hospital gown.

"Hey, Champ," he greeted Sam.

Sam paused his game to turn to Danny, his eyes sweeping over Danny's disheveled suit and hair. He clenched his jaw a little before turning back around and throwing his ball back into the air without saying a single word to Danny.

That was expected and probably deserved, but sadness still overtook Danny as Sam acted so cold to him.

"I'm really sorry about today, Sam," Danny sighed, knowing that Sam was acting that way because he was hurt. If Danny was in Sam's shoes, he would've felt the same way too.

"I waited for you all day," Sam said in a hushed voice, clutching the ball to his chest.

"I know. I feel horrible. Really, I do," Danny told him as he took a step forward toward Sam, his shoe brushing through the trimmed grass. He wanted Sam to know how sorry he was and hopefully achieve forgiveness.

Sam lowered his head, his teeth gritting briefly before he spoke again in a shaky voice.

"You never showed up, and then I found out … Janie died," he said, as he whipped around to glare at Danny, his eyes welling with tears.

Sam might as well have punched Danny in the stomach. The feeling would have been about the same, sapping the breath right from Danny's lungs. The world threatened to shift again, but he planted his feet, attaching himself to the present as much as he possibly could.

"I know," Danny said, his voice coming out weakly. He couldn't make it sound any stronger than that. There was just enough strength in his body to keep him standing up.

Sam nearly scoffed at Danny's words, his head shaking as a few tears slipped down his smooth cheeks.

"When someone dies, we need to be there for each other," he told Danny.

Before Danny could reply, Maria opened the front door of the house and stepped out onto the porch, her eyes falling on Danny.

"Come inside, Sam," she called to him, a hard expression adorning her face.

Sam sniffled before chucking the ball at Danny angrily, more tears streaming down his cheeks.

"I thought I could depend on you! Maybe I'm just a dumb kid … but I thought you were my friend!" he screamed at Danny, balling his free hand up into a tight fist.

Danny didn't even flinch as the ball caught him in the shoulder, his own eyes stinging as he watched Sam act so enraged. It wasn't like him.

"I am your friend, Sam! What can I do to make it up to you?" Danny asked, a tone of desperation accompanying his words.

Sam shook his head.

"Just be grateful ..." Sam answered dully as he turned to trudge toward the house. He paused to turn back around and look at Danny, "... you're alive." He gritted out the last part before walking up the steps to slip past Maria and head into the house.

Danny lowered his head, bringing his hand up to grip the top of it. He knew that he deserved every bit of that, but it still stung him. The one person that he thought could never hate him now loathed him.

Maria watched Sam disappear into the house before descending down the stairs of the porch to head over to Danny, her expression straight and firm.

"Gee, you're only six hours late," she commented to him sharply as she stopped a few feet in front of him, her arms crossing over her chest.

"I can explain ..." Danny started to say until Maria cut him off with a shake of her head.

"Don't bother. I've never seen him more excited than when he woke up today, even knowing he had to go through that procedure at the hospital, thinking you'd be there," Maria snapped at him, her eyes narrowing.

Danny felt more guilt wash over him as he imagined that, knowing that Sam had been looking forward to everything that Danny had promised him.

"Please, let me just ..." he tried to speak again, but Maria wasn't hearing him.

"No. Let me explain something to you. I don't recognize my son anymore. He's not the same playful, energetic boy he used to be. He knows words he shouldn't know ... tumor, biopsy, chemo. His friends are nurses and doctors," Maria reeled off, moving forward to invade Danny's space.

Danny couldn't even bear to meet her gaze, and he dropped his eyes like he was back in the courtroom. However, instead of sparing him like last time, she was ripping him to shreds, and he couldn't find it in him to try to stop her.

"Kids won't play with him when he's home because ... they don't want to 'catch' his cancer. He wakes up vomiting. He's ten!" Maria shouted, her hard composure snapping as tears fell from her eyes. Her bottom lip trembled as she stared Danny down, her breaths rushing in and out of her sharply.

Danny didn't even know what to say. He could never begin to understand their pain, but he wished that he could help. He lifted his hand to reach out to her, hoping to comfort her.

Maria immediately stepped away from his hand.

"Don't!" she snapped at him, giving him a warning glare.

"Look, I ..." Danny started to apologize.

"You being at Cedars lifted Sam's spirits, but you figured out a way to screw that up," Maria growled at him, a disappointed look gracing her face.

"Maria, listen I ..."

"Bye, Danny," Maria cut him off, her tone having a sense of finality to it. She whirled around to storm away, slamming the door of her house behind her.

Clenching his jaw, Danny kicked at the air, overcome with disgust for himself. He had done this. He hadn't been strong enough to keep himself on track, and he had ruined everything. He just wanted to stop messing everything up, but destruction was his constant curse.

Danny found himself back in Dr. Vanowen's office the next day, lying on a leather recliner instead of sitting at Dr. Vanowen's desk. Dr. Vanowen sat next to Danny while taking notes on a notepad.

"... he looked like any old man over there ... a long dark robe, head scarf ... he could barely walk, and he was carrying a couple loaves of bread ..." Danny trailed off as he told the story, his voice shuddering as he spoke. He gripped the end of shirt anxiously, forcing his shaky hands to grab onto something for stability. He didn't like having to go back into the past on purpose, but Dr. Vanowen claimed that this would help him in the long run.

"What happened, Danny?" Dr. Vanowen lightly pressed Danny to keep talking as he peered up from his notepad, his black pen perched in his hand.

"I actually nodded hello to him. He was trying to feed his family ... in the middle of all that, but something didn't feel right. I watched him walk up the road ... and he ... dropped it," Danny said, darkness overtaking his vision despite his eyes still remaining open.

Danny was shuttled back into Iraq, his hands gripping his M-4 rifle instead of his shirt. He clutched the gun to his chest as he watched the old man drop the bag of bread in his hands before scurrying across the road and pulling out a cell phone. Danny dropped his eyes to the "bread," realizing that it looked more like a small artillery shell with wire wrapped around it.

The old man lifted his head and noticed Danny. He narrowed his eyes and backed himself up behind a wall out of Danny's line of sight.

With his heartbeat pounding in his head, Danny prompted himself to run toward the explosive device, knowing that he needed to hurry up and take care of it. Upon his first step toward the device, small arms fire rained down on him and his platoon, bullets peppering the ground and bodies.

A gasp left Danny as he returned to Dr. Vanowen's office, his eyes burning sharply as he blinked them rapidly.

"I couldn't warn 'em fast enough. I tried … I yelled …" Danny said in a hushed voice, unable to make his voice come out any stronger. He shook his head rapidly, tears coursing down his cheeks as he gritted his teeth so hard that his jaw ached. It physically pained him to return to those memories, to see all of that horror in front of his eyes all over again.

"It's alright … it's alright. That's enough for today," Dr. Vanowen cut in as he nodded, a sympathetic look crossing his face. He reached out to pat Danny's shoulder, trying to soothe him as much as he could.

Chapter Twelve

A slight pain graced Danny as he fell into the same pace as Markus's push-ups, his hands pressing down into the infield grass of the local high school's track.

"Twenty-four ... twenty-five," Danny puffed out as they moved, his breathing shifting in through his nose and out through his mouth.

Markus collapsed onto the ground, rolling onto his back to stare up at the blue sky up above, an exhausted sigh leaving him.

Danny followed suit, turning over to sit down next to Markus's side, sweat glistening on the crown of his head.

"That's five more than you did last week," Danny commented as he gazed off.

Heavy breaths puffed from Markus as he chuckled and nudged Danny with his elbow.

"I'm catching up to you, Vitello!" he quipped excitedly. When Danny merely sighed in response, a frown crossed Markus's face.

"What's up, partner?" Markus asked him.

"Maria and Sam won't talk to me," Danny said quietly, the pain moving inward as he listened to his own words. It felt like a piece of him was missing, one that he wasn't sure that he would ever get back now. He had messed up big, and the consequences were worse than he could ever imagine them to be.

Markus sighed as he lowered his eyes.

"That's rough, man. Ya know, with the stuff you're dealing with, maybe you could explain that to Maria. I mean, her boy's dad was in the military, right?" Markus suggested, lifting his eyebrows a degree out of curiosity.

Danny nodded, his eyes widening a little as he seriously considered Markus's words. He would do anything to be back in Maria and Sam's lives again, which could mean that he might have to open himself up in ways that he hadn't to many other people. It frightened him to bare his soul like that, but it was a risk that he was willing to take.

The slight rush of bravery that Danny had felt before with Markus nearly disappeared when he was face to face with Maria on the front porch of her house. He shifted nervously to wait for Maria's response to his extensive explanation of his issues as Maria crossed her arms and stared at him with a hard expression. He had pretty much spilled everything to her, having to force himself to speak the words that he had been too scared to tell most other people. He just hoped that she would understand what he was going through.

"I'm getting help. All these years, I'd been afraid to …" Danny added as his hands wrung themselves together in an anxious manner.

"I know you're dealing with a lot," Maria finally spoke, her expression softening a degree.

"Between the news about Janie and my agent meeting … it was just too much … I lost control," Danny explained to her, wanting her to know that it had nothing to do with her and Sam.

"I'm glad you're finally getting help," Maria said within a soft sigh, uncrossing her arms.

"I promise you that I'll never let you guys down again. Please, Maria, can you forgive me?" Danny asked her, knowing that it was a lot to ask, but he really wanted things to be good between them again. He had felt so lost in the world without them, and he didn't want to keep feeling like that. He slowly extended his hand out to her, hoping that she would take it.

Maria stared at his hand for a few seconds before taking it and shaking it in a business-like fashion, her chin tilting up.

"You're gonna have to talk to Sam," she told him as she nodded toward the front door of the house.

Danny nodded, knowing that he owed Sam an explanation, too. It was only fair.

"I'll make it up to you. I swear," Danny promised her, wanting to show how sorry he was and how important they were to him. Quietly, he let her lead him to Sam's room, his head peeking inside to gaze at Sam.

With sagging shoulders and distant eyes, Sam sat on his bed and doodled on a drawing pad quietly. A medical IV pole was stationed near his bed, while a Peter Pan action figure stood on his dresser. However, what really struck Danny was all of his own movie posters on Sam's walls.

Danny walked into Sam's room quietly, taking in the space. Everything seemed perfectly in place and representative of Sam besides the IV pole. Danny tried to ignore the fact that Sam was so sick most of the time. He wasn't just a hospital patient to Danny. He was so much more.

"Those wings I had to wear were so heavy that my shoulders are still sore," Danny commented as he pointed out his *Purple Hawk* movie poster.

Sam looked up from his drawing pad at Danny, keeping his face straight.

"My mom always says, 'You're only as good as your word,'" Sam said in a bitter tone.

Danny nodded as he stepped away from the poster to face Sam.

"She's right. And I didn't keep mine," Danny admitted, knowing that he needed to be up front and honest with Sam, even if he was only a kid. He was smarter than most.

"Why?" Sam bit out.

Danny hesitated, thinking of the best way to approach the subject. It was a heavy one, and it was even hard to explain to some adults.

"Remember when they had to operate on your brain?" Danny asked him.

Sam nearly scoffed at Danny's words as he nodded his head.

"Hard to forget *that*," Sam pointed out.

"Well, I have something wrong with my brain, too, but an operation can't fix it. My mind's the problem. I remember bad stuff … I have really bad … dreams," Danny explained, tiptoeing around a little. He didn't want to expose Sam to the really dark details. He merely wanted Sam to understand that he had struggles of his own that were out of his control at times.

"You do?" Sam asked, his face softening a little as he listened, sitting up more in his bed. His drawing pad laid discarded in front of him.

"Really bad. The day I didn't show up for you and your mom ... they were the worst yet," Danny admitted, keeping himself from shuddering at the thought. He could only hope that they didn't get any worse than that, but stress triggered his memories the most, and life had been incredibly stressful lately.

"Whenever I have bad dreams, I turn on the light and I start coloring," Sam explained as he reached into his nightstand to pull out a few coloring books. He handed one over to Danny.

"Take this one. I only colored in the first two pages," he said softly.

Danny felt something warm swell in his chest as he took the coloring book, nearly feeling choked up at the gesture. He knew that it seemed small to Sam, but it meant a lot to Danny that Sam even cared to try to help him after what Danny did.

"That is awfully kind of you, Sam. I'm gonna keep this right by my bed," Danny told him as he held the coloring book close to his chest.

A smile slowly crossed Sam's face, brightness and color flooding back to his cheeks.

"I got a doctor helping me too, kinda like how your doctors help you – a mind doctor. I'm starting to get better," Danny told Sam as he gradually approached his bedside. He reached out and took Sam's hand. "Sam, I'm truly sorry. You mean the world to me. I won't let you down again," Danny told him sincerely, having already suffered too much loss to keep losing people that meant the world to him. They were the only things keeping him going at this point. Since he treasured them so dearly, he knew that he couldn't keep letting them down.

"You done screwed up once, you ain't gonna do it again," Sam recited a line as he cracked a smile at Danny.

Danny lifted an eyebrow at Sam, giving him a confused look.

"That was from *Wolves Creek*, right before the Sheriff shot ya," Sam explained with a light laugh, shaking his head.

A chuckle sounded from Danny as realization dawned over him. It warmed him that there was someone out there who knew his lines and his roles better than he did. It meant a lot that someone as good and pure as Sam looked up to him and admired him, despite everything that Danny had done that he wasn't proud of. It motivated Danny to try to be better.

"Boy, Champ, you're good," Danny told him warmly.

Sam pointed at the *Wolves Creek* poster behind him with a proud lift of his eyebrow. A moment later, he pushed himself gradually to his feet on the surface of his bed and tossed his arms around Danny in a tight hug.

"I love you, Danny," he said.

Danny squeezed Sam to his chest, clenching his jaw to keep his eyes from watering even more. Joy swelled in his chest, glowing so bright and warm that it nearly ached, but he welcomed the feeling. He missed feeling it.

"I love you too, Sam," he breathed out, holding tight and promising to never let go.

Clapping filled the auditorium, and Danny beamed at his group of actors as they finished up a costumed rehearsal. Things were coming together well and better than he had expected. Everyone got along, putting in their all, despite many of them being exhausted or not feeling their best. He admired their determination and work ethic, hoping that this production gifted them a little spirit to get through their hard days.

"Great job today, everybody! Same time tomorrow," he called to them from in front of the stage. He turned his head to see Sam toward the right of the stage, staring down at his feet with a slump to his shoulders. Frowning, Danny climbed onto the stage and headed over to him.

"Sam, you were great today! You knew almost every line!" Danny praised him, hoping to cheer him up.

"Thanks," Sam answered automatically, not lifting his eyes.

Danny sighed as he crouched to get down to Sam's level, knowing where this sadness was coming from. He felt it himself, but he put a smile on his face for everyone else.

"I know it's hard without Janie. I wanted to do a little something with you before your mom picks you up," Danny told him, watching a hint of a glow return to Sam's eyes.

At the LA county court, Maria sat at her desk full of legal briefs in her office, chatting on her phone.

"We're not having this conversation, Stace," Maria said pointedly as she relaxed back against her rolling chair.

"Sis, why not? He treats Sam good. He's *hot* ..." Stacey's voice sounded through the phone's speaker.

"Stop! I have my reasons! Okay?" Maria declared as she tilted her head back.

"Well, give him my number then! And give my nephew a big kiss for me. Love you," Stacey replied, sounding a bit defeated.

"Love ya, too," Maria conceded before hanging up. She clicked on the photo app on her phone and started scrolling through her photos, her eyes finding one of Danny and Sam from Thanksgiving. Uncontrollably, a smile slowly crossed her face as she tapped on it, noting how happy Sam looked. She wanted to keep him that way.

— — —

Danny led Sam through a park near the hospital, pink helium balloons in their hands. He hoped that Sam would like this idea. Danny had thought about it earlier, intent on doing something special in Janie's honor.

"So, we each write a message to Janie on our balloons, and then we'll release them at the same time," Danny explained to Sam as he took two felt tip markers out of his pants pocket. He held one out to Sam, who was far more animated now than earlier.

"I like that!" Sam exclaimed as he took the marker from Danny's hand. He steadily wrote on his balloon, creating the message "I miss you!" on it.

Danny held his balloon tightly so that it wouldn't move, tracing his marker over its surface until it popped in his hands. He flinched, a frown crossing his face.

"You can write something on my balloon, Danny," Sam offered kindly as he handed Danny his balloon.

"Thanks," Danny told him gratefully before writing out "Me too" with a smiley face on the balloon. He placed the balloon back in Sam's hands and nodded.

"Whenever you're ready, Sam," he announced, tilting his head up toward the sky.

With a deep breath, Sam released the balloon, his eyes trailing it as it floated quickly toward the sky up above, a smile brightening on his face. Before they knew it, the balloon had disappeared.

Heavy huffs left Danny as he slowed his run down to a walk, his sneakers thudding against the surface of the high school's track. He lifted his hands up above his head, taking in a few deep breaths to calm his heart rate. He didn't mind the ache, liking that it was something he could manage and control. As he dropped his hands, he spotted a female approaching him from the opposite way, her body adorned in a pink track suit and sneakers. As she came closer to him, realization struck him.

"Angie?" he inquired as they continued to walk toward each other until they faced one another.

"Had a hunch you might be here," Angie commented as she rested her hands on her hips.

Danny hesitated before answering, having been caught off guard.

"Everything okay?" Danny asked her, tilting his head a little. He wondered why she wanted to find him in the first place.

Angie shrugged lightly, a faint smile crossing her lips as she gazed at him.

"Just wanted to catch up. You look good," Angie told him warmly.

Danny glanced down at the ground briefly, his mind full of swarming thoughts. So much had changed since they had last seen each other. He still didn't know how to properly act around her at this point. He wasn't sure if he would ever figure it out.

"You too," he managed to say, shifting awkwardly on the spot.

Angie drew her hand through her hair, pushing a few loose strands back from her forehead as she took a step closer to him.

"How are things at the hospital? Markus and Lydia were saying …" she started to explain until Danny cut in.

"Yeah, they told me that they ran into you. The hospital was supposed to be punishment, but it ended up being … pretty great. Our show's tomorrow night," Danny told her, the side of his mouth curling up just slightly in a smile at the thought. He had worked hard on the show, and it had all been worth it.

Angie nodded, giving him a proud look that made his chest tighten.

"I got your email … it made me happy. I'm glad you're getting help," Angie told him sincerely, her eyes resting on his for a few tense seconds until she spoke up again to break through the silence that had settled between them.

"I miss you."

Danny blinked a few times, not expecting to hear her say that to him. He felt his heart start to race, his words threatening to get trapped in his throat as he stared at her. He almost thought that he had imagined her saying those words. He had done that already before in his daydreams.

"I miss you too. I …" he started to say until Angie broke him off with a gentle kiss. He didn't move, and neither did she, remaining joined for a few seconds by a warm touch. Danny didn't want it to end, but she eventually pulled away from him.

"I better go," Angie told him, a light red flush crossing her cheeks as she steadily backed away from him. At his nod, she turned and strode away, leaving him in a daze. She looked back at him with a bright smile.

"Merry Christmas!" Angie called to him.

Danny merely smiled back, unable to think of anything to say. He just watched her go, pure adoration filling him whole.

Chapter Thirteen

Maria gazed at herself in the mirror of her local hair salon, "Pretty Lady," watching two hair stylists observe her hair. She hadn't been here in a while, and she figured that it was time to fix herself up and look nice for once, especially since it was the opening night of the show at the hospital.

"Honey, you are way overdue. We'll fix you right up," one of the hair stylists assured her, flashing the other stylist a determined look.

It didn't take long for them to make her hair bouncy and shiny as it streamed past her shoulders. After an abundance of thank you's, Maria headed to the nail salon down the street, "Nailed It," and directed herself into a chair, treating herself to a pedicure and a manicure. She knew that if she was going to do all of this, she was going to go all out to look as close to perfect as she possibly could.

Once she arrived home, being careful not to chip a single centimeter of her freshly done nails, Maria scoured her closet for the perfect dress to wear that night. She pulled a silver one out, holding it up to her body as she gazed into the mirror. With a disappointed hum, she put it back in the closet and grabbed a red cocktail dress, holding it up as she returned to the mirror. With a smile, she nodded to herself and shut her closet door.

As she put on her eyeliner, Maria heard Sam's voice call from the living room.

"Mom, we can't be late. Danny wants the entire cast there by six p.m.," Sam shouted.

"One second, honey!" Maria called back before applying her lipstick, opting for a bold red color to match her dress. It was a holiday color, too, so it was perfect. She turned around a few times in the mirror once she was done with her makeup, looking herself up and down to make sure that everything looked perfect before heading into the living room.

Sam stood in front of a nicely decorated Christmas tree in the corner of the room, garland hanging all around the room and lights glowing from each surface and corner. He turned to see Maria walk out of the bathroom, and his expression immediately brightened.

"Wow! Mom, you look beautiful!" he gasped out.

Maria smiled warmly at him, placing her hand on his shoulder to not mess up his hair.

"Thank you, Sam. Let's get you to the show. Are you nervous?" she asked him, giving him a soft look. She would understand if he was, because she would be terrified. Being in a show was a completely different social experience than being in court.

"I thought that I would be, but I'm not. Danny said not to worry if we mess up lines because the audience won't know anyhow and to just have fun," Sam explained to her as he lifted his chin up, looking confident and excited.

Maria nodded as she rubbed his back, glad to hear that he was doing perfectly fine.

"Good advice. Don't forget it," she told him, not wanting him to get nervous at any point. It was all about fun, and she knew that tonight would be one to remember.

Backstage, Danny watched the cast scramble around in the dimly lit area to try on costumes, gather props, and rehearse their lines as Nurse Sally stood at his side. He ran his hand over the lapels of his black suit jacket and tie, smoothing everything down mindlessly. He wanted the production to go well, but he also just wanted everyone to enjoy themselves. This show was a break from reality for all of them.

Maria entered the backstage area with Sam at her side, his costume in his hands. She led him toward Danny, her hand moving to fluff her hair a little as they approached.

"Danny, I'm here," Sam called out to him.

Danny turned around to face them, his jaw nearly going slack as his eyes landed on Maria.

"Hey, you two!" he greeted them, unable to pull his eyes away from Maria and how incredible she looked. She always looked great, but she seemed to glow tonight. Out of the corner of his eye, he spotted Nurse Sally stepping forward, knocking him out of his mesmerized daze.

"Uh, Sally, we have to get Sam in his costume," he told her, nodding his head to Sam.

Nurse Sally smiled to herself before motioning for Sam to follow her.

"Come on, Sam, you can change back here," she told him warmly as she led Sam away.

"Okay, see ya later, Mom," Sam called to Maria as he walked off, lifting his hand in an excited wave.

"You're gonna be great, Sam!" Maria called back, a look of pride crossing her face as she watched Sam leave with Nurse Sally. She noticed Danny looking at her again, but she merely smiled in response, her face gradually warming.

"Wow! You look amazing," Danny told her as he stepped closer to her, his heartbeat sounding in his head. He couldn't bring himself to look away from such a beautiful sight.

"Wow yourself," Maria laughed softly, dropping her gaze bashfully for a moment before glancing toward the exit. "I better take my seat," she said with a blush, figuring she should get out of the way as the cast prepared.

"And I gotta, you know, get back to the … see ya later," Danny cut himself off with a faint laugh, feeling a slight burn in his face as he smiled at her, watching her strut off. He sighed wistfully, his eyes trailing her all the way until she disappeared.

"Hi, Danny."

With a shocked look, Danny whipped around to see Angie standing there, his heart jolting at the sight of her. He hadn't expected her to be here.

Angie lifted her dark glasses from her eyes to push them above her forehead, giving him a soft smile.

"They said you were back here," she told him.

Danny cleared his throat, mentally kicking himself to hurry up and say something. He couldn't stand the awkward silence.

"I didn't know … didn't think you were coming," Danny stumbled over his words, still in shock that she was actually standing there in front of him.

"And miss your first directional debut?" Angie smiled at him with a shake of her head. She turned her head to glance in the direction that Maria had exited.

"Lucky girl," she noted as she looked back at Danny, who remained silent, merely staring at her. She leaned toward him, brushing her lips against his cheek before pulling away.

"Break a leg," Angie told him warmly.

Danny nodded, managing to smile at her.

"Thanks, Ange," he said quietly, knowing that she was being genuine. Maybe she did still care about him, in a way, after all.

Angie lowered her glasses back down to cover her eyes before turning to walk away, leaving Danny stunned once again on the spot.

"Hey," Danny blurted out, not even knowing where he found the boldness.

Angie glanced back over her shoulder at him.

"Merry Christmas," Danny told her, returning the sentiment from their last encounter. She just kept popping up in his life. He wasn't sure how to feel about that just yet.

Angie smiled before continuing to walk off, Danny's eyes following her.

From behind Danny, Markus strode up to him, patting his hand against Danny's shoulder to snap Danny out of his trance.

"I'm ready for my close up, Mr. Vitello," Markus quipped playfully.

Danny smirked and shook his head as he greeted Markus, glad to have a distraction from the conflicting mess of thoughts in his head.

"Hey. You are looking sharp, my friend. Thanks for doing this," Danny told him gratefully, having dragged Markus away from the television to come to his play.

Nurse Sally walked by Danny and Markus, her eyes zeroing in on Markus, prompting her to dash over.

"I love every one of your films," she gasped out, an excited look crossing her face.

"Thank you, Darlin'. See, Danny, I still got it," Markus chuckled, shooting Danny a joyful look before turning to see Sam wandering over in his green costume.

"You are one fly looking Peter Pan there, sport," Markus told Sam warmly.

Sam stopped in his tracks, a look of realization coming over his face as he stared at Markus in awe.

"I know you! You played Danny's police chief in *Drop a Dime*."

Markus glanced over at Danny with an impressed look on his face, his eyebrows lifting slightly.

"You weren't lyin'. He does know all your movies!" Markus told him.

Danny smiled and nodded, shooting Sam a wink before glancing around at the backstage area, which was full of chaos. The cast darted each and every way, nearly running into each other as they did last minute touch ups to props and costumes. He was used to the craziness, and he realized how much he missed it. The tension before the show was high, but it didn't frighten him. It only inspired him.

"Okay, everyone! Fifteen minutes to curtain!"

A full house occupied the auditorium, a few familiar faces sprinkled throughout, including Lydia, Mrs. Schwartz, nurses, Dr. Kumar, and others. The curtain slowly dragged open, a spotlight illuminating Markus as he stood in the center of the stage with a microphone in his hand. The audience recognized him quickly, prompting them to break out into applause and cheers.

"Welcome, everyone. Thank you for attending Cedars-Sinai's Nineteenth Annual Holiday Show," Markus's voice boomed throughout the auditorium. After giving his introduction, he stepped off of the stage, and the show began, music and lights filling the stage.

Sam, as Peter Pan, spoke to Wendy, standing near her side.

"Promise me one thing … leave Hook to me," he told her, utilizing the same dramatics that he witnessed on screen in each scene that he was in.

Two other cast members playing as Peter Banning and Rufio bounded onto the stage for their scene.

"Someone has a severe ka-ka mouth, you know that?" Peter scoffed as he crossed his arms over his chest.

Rufio pointed his finger in Peter's face as he stepped close.

"You are a fart factory, pimple-squeezing finger bandage. A week-old maggot burger with everything on it and flies on the side," he sneered right back.

The audience busted out into laughter, the sound echoing throughout the entire auditorium. Maria clapped her hands happily, having a blast as she watched the show, her heart racing each and every time her son walked out on stage.

Danny stood backstage in the wings, his arm around Sam's shoulder as they watched the show from the side. He couldn't help but feel incredibly proud of how it was going so far. Even the girl who took over for Janie, she was good, but Danny couldn't help the sadness he felt that Janie couldn't have been here. Everyone was doing an awesome job, putting their all into their performances. He felt like being assigned to the hospital was far from a punishment at this point.

Sam smiled brightly as he impatiently shifted on the spot, ready to get back out on stage. He scanned the audience, spotting his mother smiling as she watched the show. To Sam's delight, his scene was up next.

Captain Hook and Sam faced each other on stage, engaging in an intense sword fight. They locked swords and scowled at each other.

"If I were you, I'd give up," Captain Hook recited his line, his lips moving beneath the fake mustache on his face.

"If you were me, I'd be ugly," Sam quipped back before diving back into the fight, the audience erupting into laughter.

Maria placed her hands over her mouth, watching her son duck and move across the stage with a proud smile on her face.

Sam rested back against a fake boulder as Captain Hook towered over him, pretending to pant as he gazed up at his nemesis.

"And now, Peter Pan, you shall die," Captain Hook growled as he pointed his hook at Sam in a threatening manner.

"To die ... will be an awfully big adventure," Sam replied as he tilted his chin up, refusing to look scared.

Captain Hook lifted his hook, preparing to finish Peter Pan off, but he stopped when he felt a tap on his shoulder. With a confused look on his face, he whirled around to see a man in a crocodile costume standing behind him. He wrestled with the crocodile, giving Sam the opportunity to escape as the crocodile took Captain Hook down to end the show.

The entire cast soon poured out onto the stage, throwing their arms around each other as the audience clapped and cheered for them. Sam moved to stand on a raised platform, placing his hands on his hips and lifting his head high in Peter Pan's iconic pose, taking in the praise.

Markus walked onto the stage with a microphone in his hand, clapping his free hand against his other wrist.

"Thanks for coming, everyone! Let's give a big hand to all of our actors who worked so hard!"

Maria, Lydia, and the rest of the audience moved to stand, continuing to clap and cheer as the actors onstage bowed.

"I wanna bring out someone y'all know, who put his whole heart into this production, my good friend, Danny Vitello. Come on out, Danny," Markus announced, motioning for Danny to come out of the wings.

As the audience and the cast cheered for him, Danny stepped out onto the stage, taking a bow in front of the audience before clapping for the cast and giving them a proud look. With the spotlight shining down on him, Danny felt like he was in a dream, his eyes moving to Sam to give him a warm smile. This night was special in more ways than just one.

After most of the people filed out of the auditorium, Danny stood next to Sam in front of the auditorium's back wall, gazing at a plaque with a photo of Janie on it. Below her photo was an inscription that read "*In Memory of Janie Holt.*" Danny moved to put his hand on Sam's shoulder, a soft sigh drifting from him. He wished that Janie could've been here to play in the show. He knew that she would've loved every second of it.

"She would have been real proud of you tonight," Danny said to Sam in a gentle voice, knowing that Sam was still sensitive to the topic.

Sam nodded quietly, turning his head to smile at Danny, a look of belief in his eyes.

Once Sam headed off to change out of his costume into a T-shirt and pants, Danny made his rounds, saying goodbye to some of the kids and their parents before they left. He thanked each and every one of them sincerely, grateful for all of their hard work. They were all strong in more ways than one.

"Mom, we should ask Danny to come over tonight," Sam told his mother as they headed Danny's way from backstage, a mischievous look crossing his face as he looked toward Danny.

"Oh, I don't know, Sam," Maria hesitated, almost looking a hint shy.

"But it's Christmas Eve!" Sam pushed a little more, giving her a pleading look.

Maria glanced over at Danny again, watching him take down a few Peter Pan decorations with a small smile on her face.

"He probably has plans already," she replied, sounding like she was arguing more with herself than with Sam at that point.

Sam reached over and took her hand, giving it a squeeze.

"Only one way to find out," he pointed out with a subtle lift of his eyebrows. He gave her a nudge in Danny's direction with an encouraging look on his face.

Maria hesitated for a moment, a sense of shyness gracing her as she looked back over at Sam, wondering if he was really going to make her do this. When he motioned for her to go with a pointed look, she walked closer to Danny, turning to shoot one more questioning look at Sam, who crossed his arms firmly. There was no going back now.

"Tonight was so much fun!" Maria commented as she joined Danny's side.

Danny nearly jumped as Maria's voice sounded next to him, his head turning to gaze at her with slight surprise. It soon melted into warmth as he smiled and nodded.

"Sam was great. It's gonna feel strange not coming back here every day," Danny said, finding himself missing this place and everyone in it already. It had become a sort of home to him, welcoming him in and making him feel worth something. He felt like he could be a good person here and do good things, while the outside world remained daunting.

"I'm sure everyone is going to miss having you around, especially Nurse Sally," Maria replied as she brought her hands together in front of her, her fingers twining together in a nervous manner.

"Wouldn't have been able to pull it off without her," Danny chuckled, feeling thankful for everyone who helped him put the show on. He couldn't have done it alone, and he wouldn't have wanted to when there were so many great people here.

Maria shifted nervously on the spot as she coaxed herself to speak again.

"Sam was ... well, *we* were ..." Maria trailed off as she glanced back over her shoulder at Sam again, who waved her on.

"... wondering if you're free tonight. We'd love for you to stop by for some Christmas desserts," Maria finished, feeling her heart thud heavily against her chest.

Danny blinked a few times in surprise, not expecting the offer, but he couldn't deny the happiness that flooded through him at receiving it.

"That sounds ... yes. Great, I just ... wouldn't want to intrude or anything like that," he told her, not wanting her to think that she was obliged to do anything for him. He wanted her and Sam to be fully comfortable with him and to invite him only if they were one hundred percent certain about it being something that they wanted to do.

Maria shook her head at him with a small smile.

"You wouldn't be. At all. Okay, then ... we'll ... uh ... see you soon," she said a bit bashfully as a glowing feeling filled her, and she walked back toward Sam, who was nearly bouncing on the spot out of pure glee.

Danny stood in Maria's living room that night flipping through a few photos that Maria had given him before disappearing into the kitchen. He glanced up briefly at Sam, who sat in front of a wood burning fireplace watching television. With a warm smile, he dropped his eyes back down to the photos, which were of Sam and his mom, Sam's dad in his Army uniform, and Maria's law degree from UCLA. There was so much history there, and he wanted to know all of it. He wanted to know them.

"Your home looks beautiful," Danny voiced as he stacked the pictures into a neat pile in his hand.

"A beautiful mess, more like it. Between work, the holidays, and just *life*, we barely had time to decorate," Maria answered from the kitchen.

Danny turned to admire the Christmas tree full of various decorations and ornaments, along with the delicately wrapped presents under it. They still did a great job decorating, despite everything that had been going on.

"Looks like Santa came early, huh, Champ?" Danny asked Sam.

"Can I do it now, Mom?" Sam asked as Maria entered the living room.

"Yes, sweetie, because it's almost time for you to go to bed," Maria told him with a nod. As Sam darted down the hall, she handed Danny a soda before gesturing to the couch facing the fireplace and sitting down.

Danny moved to sit next to her, thanking her kindly for the soda as he lifted it to sip on it. He looked up as Sam rushed back into the living room with a wrapped flat square box with a bow and tag on it that read "Merry Christmas, Danny. Love, Sam and Mom."

"Merry Christmas!" Sam exclaimed as he handed the box over to Danny.

Danny's eyes widened in surprise, not expecting the gift.

"You didn't have to get me anything, Sam," Danny told him as he steadily pulled off the red wrapping paper with white snowflakes on it. He gazed down at a framed photo in his hands, one that displayed all three of them smiling on the Cedars-Sinai holiday show red carpet. He felt his chest ache with awe, his eyes even burning slightly at the thought behind the gift.

"I don't know what to say, Sam. This is one of the best gifts anyone's ever given me. Thank you," he told Sam genuinely.

"You're welcome. Nurse Sally gave me a photo printer last year for my birthday," Sam announced warmly, beaming at Danny.

Danny held the photo up so that Maria could see it better.

"That's a good-lookin' trio right there," he chuckled.

Maria smiled, warmth burning at her cheeks before she turned to Sam.

"Okay, mister, time for you to get to bed," she told him as she pulled him into a tight hug.

"Goodnight, Mom. Goodnight, Danny. Thanks for letting me play Peter Pan. Tonight was, like, the best day of my life," Sam told them, a happy look gracing his face.

"You were amazing, Sam! Thanks again for my gift. I'm gonna hang it up somewhere special," Danny promised him with a confirming nod. He was happier than he could describe about Sam saying that tonight meant a lot to him. That was all that Danny wanted to come out of this play. He wanted people to have a good time and to forget about reality for at least a little while.

Sam tilted his head up in a proud manner before striding down the hall to his bedroom.

"Watching Sam on stage was so remarkable. It's just ... I didn't know what his future might be, but after seeing him tonight ..." Maria trailed off before she got choked up, merely smiling with pride.

"He's one tough kid. You did good, Maria. His father would be proud," Danny told her sincerely, angling his body toward her more. She deserved to know that her efforts weren't for nothing. She had raised an incredible kid.

"Oh, yes. Sam reminds me so much of Frank ... his smile, his sense of humor. Sam has this look every now and then that ... it's so Frank ..." Maria sighed wistfully as she reached for a framed photo of her and Frank on the end table and showed it to Danny.

"Look at his expression. Is that Sam or what?" She laughed softly.

Danny looked closely at the familiar look on Frank's face, a small smile gracing his own as he nodded.

"He was the only love I really knew until Sam. We met in high school..." Maria said, her eyes closing momentarily as she sank back into her distant memories.

"… Frank Fleetwood. You know, before life, things were so, back then, just so innocent. We always knew we'd get married …" Maria continued, a smile crossing her lips as her eyes remained distant.

"… we were both so excited to conquer life. He was an Army Ranger like you. Frank was going to change the world for the better, and then he came home, and *he* was changed," Maria said, her voice cracking as she tried to stay composed. Her jaw tightened as she sighed, her body shuddering.

"I only recognized him in brief moments. Iraq … I don't know what happened there, but I could see he was in pain. He wouldn't get help, and I didn't know how to help him. There was nothing I could do. I mean, if there was, I would have … and then I came home one day … and he had …" Maria broke herself off with a sob, her body wilting over.

Danny caught her, drawing her to his chest and holding her tightly as she cried into his shirt.

"It's okay …" he said softly, his hand sweeping down her back in a comforting manner. It was a horror that he could somewhat understand, and it pained him what Maria and Frank had to go through. His eyes shifted to the side to look at the photo on the end table, focusing on Maria and Frank, along with his Fleetwood name tag.

Chapter Fourteen

Danny stretched his arms up over his head, panting lightly as he and Markus winded down from their laps. It was getting easier and easier for him to do this, his body becoming used to the exertion. It was an easier ache to manage than emotional pain.

"I spoke with Julie Cash the other day. She's casting *The Homecoming* in a few weeks. Gonna be a good one. Not a big budget, but a great story," Markus said as he rested his hands on his hips, catching his breath as sweat tainted the front of his grey T-shirt.

"Good for her. She's a sweet lady," Danny replied with a small smile. He brought his hands back down, rolling his neck around to stretch the muscles.

"It's based on that journalist, David Blackstone. He was held prisoner and tortured by the Taliban for years and eventually escaped," Markus explained, his eyes resting on Danny.

"I was over there when that went down. Their a role in it for you?" Danny asked, lifting his eyes to meet Markus's gaze.

Markus smiled and shook his head, taking a step closer to Danny.

"Not me. You, on the other hand ..." he trailed off with an excited look.

Danny paused, narrowing his eyes slightly.

"What do you mean?" he asked, feeling his heart rate start to pick up. He tried not to get ahead of himself, but Markus had a certain tone to his voice that hinted at something.

"The lead role of David Blackstone," Markus replied.

"I'm still not following," Danny told him with a slight shake of his head.

"They cast Kendra Kastle as Blackstone's wife," Markus explained some more.

"Kendra's amazing," Danny replied with a nod, knowing of Kendra Kastle. She was well known in the industry.

"So are you, my friend, which is why Julie says they're considering you …" Markus began, but he was cut off by Danny.

"Me? They're considering *me*. Oh, really?" Danny breathed out, his eyes lowering to the ground in shock. He had been wanting to get back into the groove for so long now, and someone might finally give him a chance at last.

"They realize that you haven't worked in a while. And the baggage. But …" Markus started to explain.

"The big but …" Danny said, having expected this to hit him eventually. There was always a "but" when he came across an opportunity nowadays, and it always sent him spiraling back.

"You'd have to audition for it," Markus finished with a small frown.

A cold laugh broke from Danny as he shook his head.

"Pass," he declared before turning to start running on the track again. His breaths puffed in and out, his eyes narrowing slightly. Of course, he would have to audition just to get turned down. He had been in this position before, and he didn't want to go through it again.

"This is your chance!" Markus called out as he chased Danny down, reaching out to grab Danny's arm to force him to stop.

Danny sighed as he slowed down to face Markus.

"At what? Being ridiculed and laughed at? They wouldn't give me that role in a million years. Did you make all this happen?" Danny asked him.

Markus shrugged, his eyes dropping down to the ground.

"I made a call, sure, but ..." he stammered.

"Ya see? They're just doing *you* a favor, not me. I appreciate it, though, man," Danny sighed, reaching out to pat Markus's arm briefly. At times, it helped having someone with connections in his corner, but it didn't guarantee him success. Nothing was guaranteed.

Markus shook his head as he crossed his arms over his chest, looking disappointed.

"What are you gonna do? Direct hospital plays for the rest of your life?"

Danny shrugged with a wry smile.

"Maybe. Got rave reviews from the nursing staff," Danny quipped. At least he had fun doing that, and no one had turned him down.

"I get that you've had a few rough years, but the Danny Vitello I know wouldn't give up this easy," Markus replied, giving Danny a pointed look to straighten him out.

Danny tilted his head up toward the sky with a sigh, his eyes shutting briefly. He didn't understand why things had to be so hard sometimes. It wore him down, turned him away from even trying at times because he couldn't bear to face disappointment again and again.

"Do me a personal favor. Go in on this one, and I'll never bug ya again," Markus bargained with him, giving him a hopeful look as he stuck his hand out to Danny.

Danny held Markus's gaze for a few moments, debating on the offer. He supposed that he could stomach one more and then be done with it. He reached out and shook Markus's hand, sharing a brief smile before motioning for Markus to walk alongside him. Deep down, he was nervous, but he didn't let it show. He just had to duck his head and get through. That was all that he had control over.

Maria had lost count of how many times she had checked her reflection in the mirror while she got ready for her date with Danny. She could feel her nerves start to intensify, but she pushed them to the back of her mind, focusing on just trying to look as perfect as possible for tonight. It was a special night, one that she hoped to remember for quite a long time. A feeling of warmth surged through her chest, desire burning through her.

With her phone pressed between her shoulder and ear, she moved her eyes down the mirror to check her outfit just one more time. She didn't want it to look wrinkled or off because she moved weird or something. She wanted it to look presentable at least, prompting her to smooth her hand over her off the shoulder sweater, which hung loose on her body. She hoped that she didn't look like she was wearing a potato sack. At least her denim skirt wasn't too loose. It held tight to her hips and legs before stopping above her knees.

Her focus shot back to what Sammy was saying over the phone to her, her eyes spacing out a bit as she listened to her son speak before she replied.

"Have fun tonight, but don't stay up too late! I'll pick you up around noon, okay?" Maria spoke into the phone, smiling to herself as she listened to Sammy's reply. She hoped that he would be alright tonight and until she picked him up. It was strange being away from him, like a piece of her was temporarily missing from her.

"I love you, Sammy," Maria replied softly before letting the call end. She placed her phone down on the bathroom counter for a second, her hands shooting right back up to fix the strands of her hair, trying to pat down anything that looked frizzed. She had spent so long on her hair and used a decent amount of hairspray to keep everything in place. She would not be happy if it decided to all mess up now. She didn't have time for that, because Danny would be arriving pretty soon.

Her eyes shot to her phone again as it started to ring, prompting her to quickly answer and bring the phone up to her ear so that she could talk to her sister.

"Hi, Stace," Maria answered the phone as she leaned closer to the mirror to inspect her makeup. She didn't need smudged eyeliner or cakey foundation. She could look like a mess any other time than tonight.

"Yes, he should be here any minute. He had some good acting stuff happen, so I – oh my gosh, will you stop! I'll call you tomorrow," Maria smirked as she shook her head, her laughter bouncing off of the walls of the bathroom as she listened to her sister talk.

"No, I'm not nervous! Love you! Goodbye!" Maria reeled through her goodbye before placing her phone down again. She had a little less time now, but she was grateful for the support. It gave her a little boost of confidence that she needed. She leaned forward again to swipe her thumb under her bottom lip, ensuring that her lip gloss wasn't smudging a hint.

Maria drew in a deep breath as she finally stepped away from the mirror, her hand reaching over to spritz herself with a spray of perfume just to top everything off. She nodded to herself, a sense of happiness striking her. Tonight was going to be great, and it was about to start. She could hardly believe it.

After grabbing her forgotten full glass of red wine that she had poured for herself earlier, Maria switched off the bathroom light and headed to the kitchen. Everything smelled good, creating a pleasing aroma that filled the whole kitchen. She tilted her wine glass to down half of her wine, deciding that she needed a little bit of liquid courage to kick things off. Half a glass wouldn't hurt. It would just numb her nervousness a tad so that she wasn't overcome with anxiety. She was in no way uncomfortable around Danny, but she just wanted things to go right without her saying or doing anything embarrassing.

Maria set down her wine glass before moving to add an extra layer of lip gloss, correcting any smudged spots from drinking out of her glass. She reached down to adjust her bra and sweater, accenting her cleavage and all of the curves that she had to offer. She hoped that she looked nice. She usually didn't dress in such a teasing manner, but she was full of desire tonight. She felt like she should show it at least a little bit, to tease at what could happen.

Maria merely smiled to herself, keeping herself from biting her lip out of shyness since she had just fixed her lip gloss. She figured that her makeup would get ruined one way or another tonight, but she wouldn't mind certain ways. How her makeup looked wouldn't matter if things led where she wanted them to. Her eyes lifted immediately when she heard the doorbell ring, and her heart rate accelerated when she realized that it was finally time.

After drawing in a deep, steadying breath, Maria opened the front door of her house, her eyes falling onto Danny, who looked incredibly charming and sharp as he stood there with a bottle of wine in his hand.

"Hey! You didn't have to bring anything. Come in," she invited him as she stood aside to let him pass through the door.

"Wasn't sure if you were a wine drinker," Danny told her as he stepped inside of her house, a smile wavering on his lips as his eyes swept over her figure.

"Oh, ya know, every now and then," Maria quipped as she motioned for him to follow her to the kitchen.

A small chuckle sounded from Danny as he followed her, looking toward the stove as steam rose from two big pots on the top of it. He drew in a deep breath, reveling in the savory aroma of what she was cooking.

"Whatever you're cooking smells delicious," Danny told her.

Maria smiled to herself, glad that he thought so. She had been working hard on getting everything prepared for tonight because she knew that it would be special.

"You said you loved spaghetti and meatballs. Why don't you open that bottle? There's a corkscrew in the drawer," Maria suggested as she motioned to the drawer, not minding a little more liquid courage to kick things off. She turned to grab two wine glasses, nearly running into him as he moved to grab the wine.

"I'll … go this way," Danny awkwardly laughed as he shuffled one way.

"And I'll just …" Maria broke off with a little laugh, a blush crossing her cheeks as she stepped the other way. She walked up to the top cabinet, standing up on her bare tiptoes to reach for them.

Danny glanced over at her as he opened the wine bottle, unable to draw his gaze away. She looked stunning, making his heart rate threaten to skyrocket. The loud pop of the cork snapped him back to reality, and he shook his head at himself. He smiled at Maria and took the glasses from her.

"Here, let me," Danny told her, pouring both glasses before handing Maria hers. He lifted his glass a little, mirroring her motion to start a toast. His heart hammered against his chest as she seemed to shift nervously on the spot in front of him. Despite his nerves, he couldn't take his eyes off of her.

"You look amazing," he breathed out, meaning the words.

Maria parted her lips to speak, but the words didn't come out for a moment, getting trapped in her chest. She breathed in deeply before trying again.

"Can I just tell you that I've been waiting for this," Maria finally said softly.

Danny smiled at her, the anticipation eating at him.

"Me too," he replied before clinking his glass against hers. He tilted his glass back, letting the wine rush past his lips before he set the glass down. He didn't hesitate before placing his hand on her back and pulling her closer to him.

Maria fumbled to place her glass down and switch off the stove, her hands landing on the strong curves of his biceps. She tilted her head up to look at him, feeling as if the air had been knocked from her chest.

Danny drifted his free hand through her hair, tucking a strand of her hair behind her ear. His hand trailed down to her cheek, his fingertips gracing her soft skin until they brushed teasingly at her bottom lip. With a smile, Danny leaned forward, his lips crashing against hers with an unmatched intensity.

Maria dropped a hand down to grab his, tugging him along from the kitchen to the bedroom hurriedly, their lips pressing and meeting chaotically on the way there.

Danny woke up the next morning earlier than he expected to. It was still dark outside with the streetlights casting a soft orange glow through the bedroom window onto their still bodies. He turned onto his side slowly, not wanting to wake Maria up. She was sleeping so peacefully beside him, her lips slightly parted as she faced him on her side. He smiled to himself and reached forward to gently stroke her hair, tucking a few loose strands behind her ear. She was beautiful, and he felt so at peace there with her, like nothing could hurt him or haunt him. It was the calmest that he felt in so long, and he knew that it all had to do with her and how she made him feel.

That night was the first night in a very long time that he didn't have his usual, recurring nightmares from the war. He struggled with those so much as they haunted his sleep, sending him into panicked fits. Sleep was supposed to be an escape, but his nightmares prevented him from running anywhere from his trauma. They were so hard to control and cope with, like they were an absolute curse with no cure. However, it seemed like some sort of cure was in the bed next to him. She quelled his anxiety in ways that no one else had ever done before with him. It was sort of mystical to him, in a way, because nothing else really worked all that well for him.

Maria's eyes started to slowly blink their way open, the orange glow of the streetlights illuminating their vibrant color. She hummed softly, a sleepy smile gradually crossing her pink lips as she gazed over at him. Her hair was a bit matted and messy, but she still looked stunning to Danny.

"Good morning," she yawned, her voice still thick from sleep. She lifted a hand to rub at her eyes tiredly, clearing her slightly blurry vision as a small yawn broke from her lips. The memories from last night rushed back to her, filling her body with pure warmth. It was like a dream come true, but it was reality. They connected so deeply last night, and it wasn't only a physical connection. There was so much emotional tension between them that it nearly dizzied her. She hadn't felt so close to someone before, but she had known that Danny was incredibly special.

"Morning," Danny whispered to her, flashing her a warm smile as he moved a little closer to her, his arm draping itself over her hip. They were tucked under the sheets of the bed, their legs tangling beneath them. He found himself not wanting to move from the spot at all. It sounded like paradise to just stay there and lay with her all day.

"Last night ... was amazing," Maria told him, hoping that he felt the same way as she did. She had been blown away by his affection and care, how he held her so close last night. She would remember those moments and sensations forever, like they were embedded in her skin. The ghost of his touches kissed her skin even now, making her smile to herself wistfully.

"It was perfect. You were perfect," Danny replied, his other hand coming over to gently caress her cheek. His thumb drifted over her skin in an adoring manner, stroking faint lines. He had a lot of hopes for last night when he had first arrived, but he hadn't been entirely sure if they would ever happen. Even now, he was still in complete disbelief that it had happened. How did he get to be with such a beautiful girl? It blew his mind still.

"I could get used to this ... waking up next to you," Maria admitted to him, nearly wincing when she heard her own voice. She hoped that she

161

hadn't been too forward, but she wanted to be honest about her feelings. Waking up with him had already made her entire day. She felt like nothing could ruin her day at this point, because she had started it out on a perfect note. She wouldn't mind doing this all of the time, because his smile was brighter than the morning sun.

Danny nearly had to draw in a deep breath at her words, his heart seeming to swell in the depths of his chest as he leaned forward to rest his forehead against hers.

"I could, too. I could get used to doing a lot of things with you," he chuckled softly, earning a little laugh from her. He nuzzled his nose against hers adoringly before pecking it with his lips, coaxing more shy laughs from her. He could listen to her all day long, could kiss her all day long. She was bordering on being a drug for him, addicting him to no end because he didn't want to stop.

"Let's just lay here together forever," Maria sighed wistfully as she placed her hand on the back of his neck. She knew that they couldn't actually do that. They had their own separate lives to attend to, but the thought of just staying here in this bed with him highly appealed to her. She could hide from every trouble in her life by remaining here in his arms.

"Let's do it," Danny replied with a soft chuckle. He met her eyes for a few moments, sinking into their alluring depths. It felt like a magnet effect took place between them, drawing him forward until his lips collided with hers. He kissed her softly and slowly. Last night had been frantic and passionate, but he wanted to take his time to kiss her now. There would be plenty of time for other things later. For now, he wanted to take it slow.

Maria let her eyes flutter shut as he kissed her gently, her lips moving against his in soft motions. She leaned into his touch as he caressed her cheek, holding her close. She could feel her heart pound against her chest, threatening to nearly break out. Despite it being soft and slow, the moment still felt incredibly intense, burning through her like fire.

Danny tilted his head a little, better capturing her lips as they fit together like puzzle pieces. It did feel like something had been missing in his life before he found her. She made everything seem to fall into place, and he didn't want to move from the spot. He just wanted to lay there and kiss her until the orange glow of the streetlights turned into the warm haze of the morning sun.

Chapter Fifteen

At World Endeavors Agency, Max leaned back in his office chair with his phone on speaker.

"So, here's the deal with *The Homecoming*. It turns out the producers want to see a few actors to check the chemistry with Kendra," Max stated, his hand drifting down his suit jacket to smooth it down.

"Did you tell them me and Kendra have worked together before?" Brett's voice sounded over the speaker.

Max sat up in his chair, his expression looking calm and straight.

"Of course, but there's a lot of buzz about this one. I say we just play the game. There's no one in this town they're going to pick over you, anyhow," Max replied in an assuring tone.

"Whatever. I'll go in and read. It'll make me look like a team player," Brett said in an annoyed manner.

"That's my boy!" Max chuckled before hanging up. He grabbed a cigar from a container on his desk and lit it up before sinking back into his chair, letting the smoke disappear into the air.

Danny and Sam sat side by side on an examination table in a stark white room, talking quietly to one another.

"… if we started dating, with your permission of course," Danny finished his explanation, a hint of nervousness gracing him as he waited for Sam's response. After what happened with Maria, Sam deserved to be clued into what could possibly happen next. Plus, Danny cared about Sam's opinion and wanted to hear it before he moved forward with anything.

"You and my mom?! Heck yeah! That's what I've been hoping for!" Sam gasped out, looking completely shocked as he gaped at Danny.

Nurse Sally entered the room, a happy smile gracing her face as her eyes laid on them.

"Wow! My *two* favorite actors are back!" Nurse Sally quipped joyfully as she moved to stand in front of them.

"Hi, Nurse Sally! My mom has court, so her *boyfriend* is gonna watch me today," Sam told her, enunciating the word "boyfriend" with a bright smile to make Danny's face burn.

Nurse Sally smiled in surprise as she turned to look at Danny, lifting her eyebrow at him.

"Her boyfriend, huh?"

"I'm *really* here because I missed the delicious hospital food," Danny whispered to Nurse Sally as he leaned toward her.

"Well, we just have a few tests to run, then I'll see what grub I can round up for you two. First, I'm gonna need some blood from ya, Sam," Nurse Sally told him with an apologetic look.

Sam nodded with a sigh as he tugged his shirt off of his body, revealing his black and blue bruised arms, the color muddling together into a painful hue.

Danny frowned at the sight, his eyes lifting to Sam's in a worried look that Sam immediately noticed and waved off.

"It's okay, Danny. It's from the chemo. Dr. Kumar says it'll go away," Sam assured him with a small smile, not wanting him to worry.

Danny forced a smile onto his face, still feeling wracked with concern. The bruises were so dark, like the ache was deep. He hoped that it didn't hurt all that bad. He reached out and rubbed Sam's head gently, doing it for Sam's comfort as well as his own.

Nurse Sally glanced over at Danny and gave him a comforting nod, quietly letting him know that it was okay. Everything was okay. After Sam's blood was taken, Nurse Sally led them into an X-ray exam room, getting Sam set up in an MRI tube. She guided Danny into another room behind a panel of glass.

Sam remained rigid and still inside of the tube, his eyes wide in fright. He clenched his fists to try to keep himself from shaking, feeling as if there was limited air in the tight space.

"Okay, Sam, we're about to start. Just fifteen minutes this time," Nurse Sally informed him gently through a speaker. She hit a button to start the machine, and a loud banging noise sounded from it.

Sam gritted his teeth and shut his eyes, a tear breaking from one of them and rolling down his face. He breathed in shakily, wishing that he was anywhere but there.

Danny stared up at the ceiling of Dr. Vanowen's office as he laid back on the recliner, his hands resting together on his chest. He could feel his own heartbeat as it slammed repeatedly in his chest over and over. He didn't want to be doing this, but he held on to the hope that this would help him in the long run.

Dr. Vanowen sat across from Danny, reading a few lines that he had jotted down on his notepad.

"At our last session, you said you saw the explosive device, and you tried to warn *them*. Who, Danny?" he asked as he lifted his eyes to peer at Danny.

Danny shook his head as he felt his mind drift in time, wishing that he didn't have to go back, but he slipped anyway.

Back in Iraq, Danny dove behind a burnt out car, his body crashing into the dirt and sand as gunfire struck all around him. He gritted his teeth, waiting for a bullet to pierce his body, but he didn't feel any pain. At that point, he couldn't feel anything but his heartbeat in his chest.

Danny carefully peeked over the hood toward the IED, his eyes landing on a Humvee heading toward it. Narrowing his eyes to see better, he saw Elvis behind the wheel. He scrambled out from behind the car, not even caring if anyone was pointing a gun at him. He had to stop that Humvee. He waved his arms wildly as it continued to approach.

"IED! IED!" he shouted, the loudness of his voice grating against his throat.

A loud boom rattled the very earth beneath Danny's feet, throwing him backwards. His face roughly struck the ground as he rolled to a stop, his body aching from the impact. A shrill noise rang in his ears as he slowly lifted his head, dazed and dizzy. When his vision slightly straightened out, he saw Elvis writhing in pain on the ground, prompting him to push himself to his feet so that he could stumble over to him.

Elvis slumped on the ground on his stomach, pained moans sounding from him. He groaned louder as Danny carefully rolled him onto his back, blood and gashes gracing nearly every inch of his visible skin. His uniform was ripped and stained, but his nametag was still intact, reading as "Vitello."

"No! God! No!" Danny sobbed as his shaky hands grabbed at Elvis's shoulders, knowing that he couldn't piece him back together, that Elvis was broken and bloodied beyond repair. It had all happened so fast, too fast.

Elvis gazed up at Danny, a small smile crossing his face. He was still in pain, but he seemed to briefly block it for Danny, pushing through to soften his pained expression.

"Hey ... big brother ... I almost made it outta here, huh?" he breathed out painfully, struggling to get the words out. He grimaced, his body shuddering with agony.

Tears coursed down Danny's cheeks, cutting through the dirt and blood coating his skin. He couldn't get any words out. He was only able to lean down and hug his brother tightly to him until he felt his body go still. Gritting his teeth so hard to the point that it hurt, Danny didn't let go, refusing to part from him just yet. He laid there and cried so hard that his head hurt, the sounds of war and death surrounding him on all sides.

Danny felt himself get shuttled back to the present, a soft gasp leaving him as he tried to ground himself back to the present. His tears were still real as they trailed down his face.

"It's my fault! My kid brother," he whimpered, his body shaking as he tried to distance himself from that memory. However, it was the hardest one for him to get away from.

Dr. Vanowen stared at Danny silently, taking it all in before nodding and speaking.

"Listen to me, son. Your brother's death didn't happen because of *you*! You did the best you could do," Dr. Vanowen told him firmly.

"I signed up right after he did. I always watched after him," Danny said quietly, tears continuing to break from his eyes. He had let Elvis down. He had let everyone down.

"Elvis would not want you to blame yourself. He knew how much you loved him. *Do him proud!* That's what he would want," Dr. Vanowen replied as he reached out to put his hand on Danny's shoulder in a comforting motion.

Danny took in the touch, trying to draw from its gentleness and comfort. He wanted to make Elvis proud of him because he knew that he hadn't been doing a good job of that lately. Shame filled him, but he fought it off, trying to focus on the slight feeling of motivation that graced him. He just knew that he had to take it and run with it.

That night in his bedroom at Markus's house, Danny laid in bed, surrounded on all sides by pure silence. Two wooden nightstands bordered the bed. On one of them, there was a triangle framed American flag, along with a photo of Danny and Elvis in Iraq. Their arms were slung over each other's shoulders as they kept each other close, a sparkle in Elvis's eyes. The other nightstand had the framed photo that Sam had gifted him at Christmas, along with Sam's coloring book.

Danny dragged his eyes away from Sam's gift to look down at *The Homecoming* script that was nestled in his hands, while Buddy laid beside him, lashing his tail slowly. He sighed softly, knowing that he still wanted to give the audition his all. He owed himself this chance, and he needed to take it with every ounce of determination that he had.

The next day, Danny was at Maria's house after she and Sam were kind enough to offer to run lines with Danny. He stood opposite from Sam in the living room, while Maria sat on the couch with a script in her hand, watching the boys with a look of awe.

"... you're an American spy!" Sam cried out as he pointed at Danny with narrowed eyes, becoming immersed in the role in a way that made Danny proud.

"No, I'm an American journalist!" Danny snapped back, slipping into his role and acting his heart out, despite not even being at the audition yet. He missed this, falling into a role and making it his own. He hoped that he would have the chance to do that with this part, which he particularly enjoyed. After staring Sam down for a moment, he turned his head along with Sam to look at Maria.

Maria gave them a thumbs-up, an impressed look gracing her face at how into their characters they were when they rehearsed.

Sam turned back to Danny with a serious look.

"Danny, when you go audition, make sure you remind them ..." he trailed off in a dramatic manner.

"About what, Sam?" Danny wondered, giving Sam a confused look when he didn't finish his sentence.

"That Danny Vitello is BACK!" Sam exclaimed with an enthusiastic punch of his fist.

Maria clapped as she laughed to herself, watching Sam attempt to hype Danny up.

Danny lifted his hand to high five Sam, an amused look crossing his face as he shook his head playfully. He hoped that was the case, but it was up to the executives of the film. The only thing that he could do was to give it his all, and he wanted to for Sam and Maria, who remained by his side as he always would with them.

The L.A. County courtroom was full of tension as Maria paced in front of a full jury box of twelve jurors and two alternates in a dark blue power pantsuit. She looked like a predator on the prowl, her eyes shifting between the people steadily as her voice rang out.

"You've heard the witnesses and the evidence. The defense wants you to believe their client acted in good faith. Hardly," Maria scoffed the last part as she strode across the tile floor. She had hit her groove, owning the courtroom and stealing the attention away. All eyes were on her, which was exactly what she wanted. She needed them to listen to each and every word that came out of her mouth.

"The *law* must dictate our course. And today, *you* are the law!" Maria announced as she stared the jury down with a determined look on her face. She wanted them to take her side, to believe what she said and nothing else. She turned her head to look at the judge on his bench.

"The prosecution rests, your Honor," she finished up with a nod of her head.

The judge slammed his gavel down.

"The court is in recess for five minutes," he announced, his deep voice booming throughout the courtroom.

Maria walked over to her side to sit down next to her male associate, who looked ecstatic with Maria's performance. Once she sat down at the desk, Maria's eyes shifted to her phone, which lit up as it started to ring. She reached forward and plucked it off the desk to answer it.

"Hello? Hi, Dr. Kumar," Maria replied, sitting up in her chair as she listened to his words intently. Her body grew more and more tense with each passing minute, a pained expression filling her face as she shook her head desperately.

"But how?" she gasped out, her eyes burning painfully with hot tears. After listening for another few minutes, she hung up, slowly lowering the phone back down to her desk. Her eyes grew distant, tears swimming in the bottom of them before they spilled out to dart down her cheeks. With a sniffle, she buried her face in her hands, her body trembling with despair.

Danny stared out of the window of his Uber, his script clutched in his hands as he watched the city blur past him. He was on the way to his audition, his mind full of rapid thoughts. This was his chance, but it could either be one for success or yet another for failure. He wasn't sure how many more times that he could stomach failure.

The young man driving him lifted his eyes to the rearview mirror, a look of recognition filling his face at the sight of Danny.

"Hey, aren't you ...?"

"I hope so," Danny replied, his eyes remaining on the window. He hoped that he was still that notable actor, but he had been dormant for so long. Danny wasn't even sure if he still existed, but he supposed that there was only one way for him to find out.

In the casting room at Warner Bros. Studios, casting director Julie Cash, a strong-willed woman in her forties, and a few producers watched Brett and Kendra Kastle conclude their audition. Kendra seemed to glow as she performed, being in her thirties with auburn-colored hair that fell around her perfect face. Her skin was smooth and fair without a blemish in sight.

"... end scene," Julie announced from behind a table that she and the other producers were sitting at, papers and laptops scattered in front of them. Applause filled the room immediately as everyone smiled at each other, looking thoroughly impressed and excited.

"Amazing work!" one of the male producers cheered, looking sold on the performance that they had given.

"Piece of cake when I get to work with a pro like Kendra," Brett chuckled coolly as he waved his hand in a casual manner. He already had plenty of chemistry with Kendra, so the audition had actually been a piece of cake for him. It was almost too easy.

"What actress wouldn't want to shoot scenes with this guy?" Kendra laughed, a charming smile crossing her pink-glossed lips as she looked over at Brett. She moved forward to embrace him before letting the producers approach him and shake his hand, Julie following suit to pull Brett into a hug of her own.

A little while later, Danny walked past a few stages on the Warner Bros. lot, making his way to where he would be auditioning. With each step, more and more pressure built on his shoulders, weighing him down gradually. It almost became hard to even take a step, but he kept himself going, knowing that he needed to make it to his audition on time.

Across the way in the parking lot, Brett leaned against his Bentley, which was parked in a VIP spot. He gazed out toward the stages, having to do a double-take when his eyes landed on Danny as he walked to his audition in the casting office.

Danny found his way into the waiting room, the edge of his script nearly becoming crumbled in his tight grip. He turned his head to see a young casting assistant at a desk in front of the waiting room chairs.

"Hello, Mr. Vitello. I'll let 'em know you're here. Can I get you a water or anything?" the casting assistant asked him, a look of recognition in her eyes.

"I'm good. Thanks," Danny replied politely before he took a seat in the closest chair. He glanced down at his highlighted script for a few moments, letting the words soak into his mind once more. He couldn't count how many times he had gone over the script, trying to embed it in his mind so that he looked as prepared and as professional as possible. He glanced away when he heard his phone ding from a text notification. He glanced up at the casting assistant with a sheepish look.

"Oops. Sorry. Thought I shut it off," he explained as he grabbed his phone and looked at the screen to see a text from Maria.

Sam and I are heading over to Cedars, nothing to worry about, call when you can

A concerned look crossed Danny's face as he lowered his phone, hoping that everything was okay.

"Danny, hi!"

Danny's head shot up at the sound of Julie's voice, his hand moving to shove his phone back into his pocket. He would have to call Maria after his audition. Hopefully, they could both give each other good news.

"Come in!" Julie encouraged Danny with a wave of her hand.

Danny forced a smile onto his face, attempting to get his mind back on track. All that he could think about now was Sam. He stood from his chair and followed Julie into the casting room. He walked past the table

174

that all of the producers sat around, feeling his face start to warm up beneath the glow of the lights above him. It felt so hot in the room for some reason. His eyes shifted over to see Kendra standing in front of the table in the middle of the room as well. He was really in it now. This was the real deal.

Once Julie sat down in her seat and clasped her hands in front of her, her dark brown hair bouncing on her shoulders, she spoke aloud.

"Okay, let's do the scene where David comes back home to his wife. We'll start with Kendra's dialogue, page thirty-seven. Whenever you're ready, Kendra," Julie announced.

Danny moved to face Kendra, keeping his script at his side as Kendra lifted her script to read her lines from it.

"They told me you had died. Everyone told me to go on with my life, but I knew I'd see you again," Kendra recited, adopting a somber tone.

Danny's eyes seemed to distance themselves as he lowered his eyes down to the floor, his body remaining rigid and still. So many thoughts clashed in his head, and he did his best to reel them in and line them up. He knew that it was his turn, and that everyone was staring at him.

Julie and the other producers glanced at each other in an unsure manner, a few shaking their heads, like it was a mistake that they had invited Danny.

After a few more moments, which actually felt like an eternity, Danny lifted his eyes to gaze at Kendra, tears filling them steadily.

"Your face kept me alive. No matter what they did to me, I still saw it every day. I dreamt of you while I slept and while I was awake … your smell, your touch … our memories … they couldn't take from me," Danny whispered, his voice breaking at certain points. He felt so immersed in the moment that everything else fell away for a little while. He was just with

175

Kendra, prompting him to reach out and touch her cheek with his fingertips gently.

"You never left me. You were always with me ..." Danny said softly before leaning forward and capturing her lips in a passionate kiss.

Kendra let her eyes flutter shut as she caressed Danny's face, tears streaming down her own.

Julie lowered her eyes to her script, checking to make sure that a kissing scene was supposed to be there.

Once Danny broke away, he cupped Kendra's face, meeting her eyes.

"I may not look the same. My body weakened over the years. My friends don't see the same man they remember, but I'm still in here. My heart's the same, only stronger, with my love for you," Danny told her, his eyes still glistening a hint.

One of the male producers quickly wiped his knuckle under his eye to brush away a tear, his body scrunching back so that no one could see him.

Julie could only stare at Danny, her lips parting in awe.

"... end scene. Wow," Julie uttered, silence filling the room after her words faded off.

Danny turned to Julie and the producers as he came back to reality, a deep breath drawn in through his nose.

"Thank you for having me," he told them before heading out of the room, leaving everyone shocked and full of awe. As much as he wanted to stand there and hear any feedback, he knew that Sam needed him more.

Once he got to Sam's room at the hospital, Danny's eyes scanned the room. He saw Maria and Nurse Sally chatting with Sam, who was back in his hospital bed. The sight made a sharp pang strike his heart, and a frown threatened to cross his lips, but he fought it away when Sam looked over at him.

"Hey, Danny!" Sam greeted him cheerfully, despite being in his position.

Danny approached Sam's bedside, his hand reaching out to pat Sam on the shoulder gently.

"Hey, Champ! What are you doing back here?" Danny asked him.

Sam gingerly placed his hand on his stomach with a small shrug.

"I was having bad stomach pains, so they ran tests. They think it's my liver. Right, Mom?" Sam asked her as he looked her way. She stood a few feet away with Nurse Sally.

"That's right, sweetie," Maria replied, forcing a smile onto her face, while her eyes looked somber and haunted.

Danny playfully nudged Sam.

"Well, we're gonna get you outta here soon," Danny told him, hoping that would be the case. He didn't know what was up with Sam, but he suspected that it wasn't anything good, telling from Maria's face.

"Sam, I'm gonna talk with Danny," Maria said quietly as she moved toward the door of Sam's room.

"You're coming back, right, Danny? I want to hear about the audition!" Sam exclaimed, an excited look adorning his face.

"Be right back, Sam," Danny replied with a nod, promising him that he would be back. He wouldn't dare leave Sam's side if Sam wanted him there. He shot Sam one more smile before following Maria out into the hallway. Before he could even say anything, he saw the tears coursing down Maria's face, coaxing him to throw his arms around her to bring her close to his chest.

Maria sobbed into his shirt quietly, shuddering in his arms.

"I'm really scared! I don't know what to do. The cancer's spread … I can't lose my boy! I can't," she whimpered as she grasped the material of his shirt tightly, using him for support.

Danny moved to grasp her upper arms, forcing her to look into his eyes as he spoke to her with a firm tone. He had to get through to her.

"He's going to get through this. Okay? You have to believe that," Danny told her, feeling her shake in his grasp.

"I'm trying …" Maria whimpered, her bottom lip trembling as she gazed at him.

Danny nodded, knowing that she was doing everything that she could to keep herself together. However, she was a mother, and her son was sick. He didn't expect any other response from her because he knew how much she loved Sam. He pulled her back against his chest, resorting to just holding her tightly. He knew that was the only form of comfort that he could properly give her right now. His head slowly tilted back, his eyes looking up, like he was searching for something or anything to help them.

Danny and Markus sat in the kitchen in Markus's house, eating turkey sandwiches that they had made. Danny could hardly stomach the food after hearing about Sam, but he knew that he needed to keep his strength up so that he could be there to support Sam and Maria.

"I'm sorry, man. Like they haven't been through enough. I know you got more important things on your mind, but I got a call from Julie Cash an hour ago," Markus eventually broke the silence as he set down his half-eaten sandwich, unable to keep quiet anymore.

"I hope you thanked her. I didn't really get a chance to," Danny said, his eyes not lifting as he took a small bite of his sandwich. He hadn't wanted to rush out like that, but Sam and Maria came before anything else.

"You'll get another chance on set, Mr. Blackstone," Markus replied, a warm smile appearing on his face.

Danny lurched a little, nearly choking on his sandwich as a few coughs left him.

"You're messing with me!" Danny exclaimed, unable to accept that as truth. There was no way after what happened.

"No, I'm serious! She said you left them speechless," Markus laughed out, reaching across the table to pat Danny on the arm in a celebratory motion.

Danny forced a smile on his face, knowing that he should be ecstatic about the opportunity, but his mind just wasn't in the mood for celebrating. His thoughts were elsewhere, drifting far and away from where he was now.

In Brett and Angie's backyard, moonlight streaming down on the pool, Angie emerged from the rippling blue water, droplets gliding down her skin as she exited the pool. She glanced over at Brett, who was laying down in a nearby lounge chair with a cigar in his hand.

Brett looked over at a nearby table as his phone started ringing, a smirk quirking up on his lips as he grabbed it.

"It's Max," Brett called to Angie.

"I'll refresh our drinks," Angie replied as she grabbed his empty drink glass off before walking off.

Brett nodded and answered his phone, tapping on the screen a few times as he lounged back in his chair casually.

"Hey, my man, you're on speaker. Give me the good news!" he chuckled as a bold smile appeared on his lips.

"So, Julie Cash called and, of course, they loved you ... but they decided to go another way with the role," Max spoke through the speaker of the phone, his voice coming out quieter than usual, like he was hesitant.

Brett blinked a few times in shock before a faint laugh broke from him.

"That's a good one, Max," he replied with a shake of his head, thinking it was all a big joke. He had nailed the audition.

"I wish I was joking. I'm dead serious, they ..." Max tried to speak until Brett cut him off abruptly.

"Wait a second. I saw Angie's ex when I left Julie's office. Don't *even* tell me he got it," Brett gritted out the last part, his eyes narrowing at the thought. When Max didn't respond, he sat up straight in his chair, his free hand curling into a fist.

"Max?!" Brett snapped, not liking the sudden silence. He turned the speaker off and brought the phone to his ear to speak more privately as he stood up and started to pace, fuming as he moved. He glanced behind his shoulder to make sure that Angie couldn't hear him.

"Listen to me, Max. You call them back up and let 'em know that me, Angie, and every other *fucking* client of yours will no longer be available to their studio. You got me?!" Brett growled, seething quietly.

"Brett, you know I can't just ..." Max nearly stumbled over his words until he was cut off again.

"If I were you, I'd start making some calls," Brett replied coldly as he watched Angie approach with their drinks. He put his phone down before shooting her a cocky smile as she handed him a drink.

"Good news?" Angie asked with a chirp in her voice.

Brett nodded in response.

"He's just working out the finer details," he replied casually, wanting her to think that everything was okay. He lifted his glass and clinked it with hers, hiding the rage that steadily boiled inside of him.

Chapter Sixteen

Danny, Maria, and Sam sat in Sam's room as Danny shared the news of his audition, praise immediately flooding the room.

"I knew you could do it! Maybe I can visit you when you start filming!" Sam gasped excitedly from his bed as he smiled at Danny, who sat next to Maria on a nearby couch. An IV hooked into Sam's arm, the typical hospital gown adorning his small body once again.

"Definitely, Sam!" Danny replied warmly, wanting to do something special like that for Sam when he felt better. He just hoped that would happen soon.

"We're so proud of you, Danny!" Maria told him as she nudged him with her arm, her face seeming to glow as she gazed at him.

Danny smiled at them gratefully before reaching over to grab a bag off of a nearby table. He pushed his hand inside to pull out a wrapped gift that he had been excited to give to them.

"So, I got something that I wanted to give you both. Here, Sam, you open it," Danny told him as he placed the gift in Sam's hands.

Sam tore into the wrapping paper, tossing it away to reveal a framed photo, his hands clutching it to bring it near his face so that he could inspect the picture.

"An old Army pal did some digging …" Danny started to explain once he sat down.

"There you are, Danny!" Sam gasped out as he pointed to one of the soldiers lined up in the photo.

"And if you look at the guy in the second row, right in front of me, turns out me and your dad were at Fort Benning at the same time during Ranger training," Danny finished with a small smile, still feeling disbelief himself. It really was a small world, and it struck him hard that he had been in Sam's father's company without even knowing it at the time.

Sam stared at the photo in astonishment as Maria stood up to move to his side so that she could look at the photo as well.

"What! This is so … oh my God …" Maria breathed out in shock as her jaw dropped at the sight. She gently took the framed picture from Sam's hands, her eyes venturing over it for a few more seconds before she hugged it to her chest. Tears welled up in her eyes as she kept it close, a shaky breath breaking from her.

"Mom, look! Dad and Danny together!" Sam exclaimed happily.

"We weren't in the same squad, but as soon as I saw the photo, I remembered him. We all played cards in the barracks. He always won," Danny chuckled warmly, remembering those times. There were few silver linings to going off to war, but him being able to bond with the other soldiers was one of them.

"He loved poker!" Maria laughed softly beneath her breath, still holding the picture to her chest.

"Just like me!" Sam added, gazing at them with a smile as Danny and Maria moved forward to hug Sam and kiss his head.

Once they pulled away, Danny glanced over at Maria, a strong pulling sensation growing in his chest. Unable to help himself, he leaned forward and captured her lips in a gentle kiss that made his heart flutter. With her, he had taken so many chances, putting his all into his efforts with her. There wasn't a limit to his affection, and he hoped that she could feel that with every touch and every kiss that he pressed to her soft lips.

A celebration for Danny being casted was held at Markus's house the next day. Danny and Markus stood to the side of the kitchen, beaming brightly as Lydia carried a large white frosted cake over to the wooden kitchen table in front of them. Along its top were the words *"The Homecoming – Congrats Danny!"* on the top in bright blue frosting. Lydia had started whipping it up immediately after hearing the news that Danny had been casted for the role.

"We're proud of you, Danny," Lydia told him warmly as she reached out to sweep him into a warm hug, her hands patting his back.

Danny chuckled and wrapped his arm around her back to draw her close, his lips finding her cheek in a grateful touch. It felt like his life was starting to finally take a good turn, and he had the best support system that he could possibly ask for.

"You're too good to me," Danny replied, flashing her a bright smile as he stepped back from her. His eyes moved to the cake on the table as Markus's phone started to ring, a warm feeling blooming in his chest. He hadn't felt this happy in a long time, and he liked the people in his corner. They gave him more hope for the future than he had ever felt before. Maybe there was a way out of this hole that he had dug himself.

As Lydia started to slice the cake, Markus answered his phone, immediately turning to Danny with a smile on his face.

"Yes, he's right here!" Markus spoke aloud before handing over his phone to Danny with an eager nod.

Danny narrowed his eyes slightly in confusion, not sure of who was on the other end of the line. He took Markus's phone and brought it up to his ear. Upon hearing the familiar ring of Julie's voice, his heartbeat immediately ramping up.

"Oh, hi, Julie … yes, we're actually having a little celebration. I wanted to thank you for …" Danny stopped speaking as Julie took over, his body visibly deflating with each word that graced his ear as he listened to her speak. The sunshine that once shone on him was now devoured by dark clouds, and the storm immediately set in.

"… I understand. Of course. Bye," Danny said quietly, the last word unable to make his voice come out any stronger. It felt like his words wanted to die in his throat, while his hope died in his chest.

Markus and Lydia quietly shared a look, frowns crossing their faces as they soon figured out the nature of the phone call.

Once the call ended, Danny cleared his throat and handed Markus his phone back, trying to hold himself together, despite feeling himself threaten to fall apart at the seams. He was scrabbling to keep the pieces together because he didn't want to break apart in front of his friends, who had worked so hard to celebrate what he used to have.

"Can't let this cake go to waste now, can we?" Danny said after a few moments of silence. He didn't want to fully ruin the moment, despite it not even existing anymore. He knew that Markus and Lydia were feigning happy smiles, which he was grateful for. It meant a lot to him that they were still trying for him. He knew that he needed to return the favor. He just had to find the strength to do so first.

Later that day, Danny broke the news to Sam, knowing that he deserved to know. Sam was Danny's biggest supporter and fan. Danny hoped that Sam knew that he was just as prominent in Sam's corner.

"So, you're not upset?" Sam asked with a solemn look on his face. He sat up in his hospital bed, a pale look gracing his complexion and a glassy look adorning his eyes as he gazed over at Danny, who stood at his bedside.

Danny wasn't as upset as he thought that he would be. He would've been shattered months ago, but things felt different now. Back then, he had absolutely nothing. Now, he had more than he deserved. He had Sam, Maria, Markus, and Lydia, who all cared about him with all of their hearts. He hadn't lost everything, and he held onto that thought, especially now as he weathered the storm that he was caught in.

"Nah, a few months ago, I would have been, but … there's more important things in life, right?" Danny pointed out, not wanting to drag Sam down into a bad mood. No matter what happened to Danny's career, he knew that it was nowhere near as bad as what Sam went through on a daily basis. He was the one who struggled day to day.

"Yeah," Sam agreed, still looking a bit deflated. He glanced down at his hands, his fingers looking thin and frail.

Danny watched Sam for a few moments, a frown crossing his face. He could tell that a lot was on Sam's mind, far too much for a child to worry about. It broke Danny's heart, and he wished that he could take the stress away from Sam, who didn't deserve to feel a hint of it.

"So, are you ready for tomorrow?" Danny asked him, breaking the silence that had filled the room. It was better if Sam talked about his feelings instead of bottling them up inside. Danny knew that he had no room to talk on that topic, but Sam could still be saved. He thoroughly believed that, even if Danny himself was a goner.

Sam shrugged faintly, hardly moving his thinning shoulders under the hospital gown.

"I just ... I just hope this is my *last* operation .... Can I ask you something, Danny?" Sam asked as he lifted his eyes slowly.

Danny nodded as he moved to sit on the edge of the bed next to Sam, his eyes beckoning Sam to continue.

"Of course, Sam. Anything," he replied with an encouraging nod.

Sam took a moment before speaking.

"Remember when I was Peter Pan and my line 'dying will be a great adventure?' Do you think it will be?" Sam asked sincerely, his voice faltering with each word that passed through his chapped lips, the pink having slightly faded from them.

Danny found himself clenching his jaw, trying to hide the look of pain that threatened to ripple across his face. Sam shouldn't have been talking or even thinking about death. That wasn't something for kids to worry about, yet Sam was asking him questions about it. He had so many thoughts about death himself, but they weren't to share with Sam. They were nearly far too dark for himself.

"I'm really scared, Danny. I don't want to die," Sam said, his eyes beginning to glisten as he gazed up at Danny.

Danny reached out to place his hand on Sam's arm in a comforting touch, needing to draw Sam out of his own head before he got lost there. Danny knew all about that, and he didn't want Sam to be faced with that same darkness. Reality was what he needed to focus on, and Sam was still alive. That was what mattered.

"That *ain't* gonna happen, ya hear me?" Danny replied firmly, refusing to let Sam think that his time was nearly up. He was just a kid. He had so much life left to live, so many memories to create and live out.

Sam nodded, remaining quiet as he quickly blinked his eyes in an attempt to dry them.

"But whenever our time does come … I do think it'll be an adventure … and everyone we love will be there," Danny added, not wanting Sam to be overly afraid of death. It was a natural part of life, but Danny wanted Sam to be incredibly old and die of old age, not sickness as a child. It wasn't fair. Danny was tired of being reminded that the world was unfair.

"Me too," Sam assented, his face brightening a degree as he nodded his agreement. No matter what happened, he wouldn't be alone.

Angry shouts rang across the backyard of Brett and Angie's house. Angie stomped around with her cell phone held against her ear, her eyes narrowing and her teeth gritting. Her skin felt hot, anger burning through her.

"What?! He said you were working on some finer details … you have to call them *now*! And you better make things right, Max, or I swear, I *will*. Danny deserves that part!" Angie growled out, seething angrily as she paced.

"Hey, babe," Brett's voice sounded behind her.

Angie whipped around to watch Brett walk into the background from the house with a drink in his hand. The closer that he got to her, the angrier she felt. She swallowed hard, her hand threatening to shake as she gripped the phone.

"Handle it. Gotta go," Angie stated abruptly before hanging up the phone with a hard click. She watched Brett stride over to her for a few more moments before she decided to meet him halfway. She walked up to him with determined steps, her hand soon cocking back and then lashing forward to smack him across the face.

The hallway leading to the operation rooms was nearly filled up with nurses and doctors, along with Maria, Danny, Nurse Sally, Markus, and Lydia, who surrounded the gurney that Sam laid on. Tension hung in the air, but no one showed their fears to Sam. All adopted encouraging smiles and said comforting words to him as he stiffly laid back against a pillow.

"You ready, champ?" Danny asked as he moved to Sam's side, putting on a grin for Sam. He was beyond nervous, but he didn't want to add onto the anxiety that Sam already felt. Danny knew that he was strong, that he had to make it out okay. There was no other reality that he would dare accept.

Sam nodded as he looked up at Danny, his breaths coming out slightly shaky. Unlike the rest, he looked worried, a small frown gracing his paling lips.

Danny leaned closer, his hand clutching Sam's in a comforting grip. He knew that no amount of words or smiles could make Sam feel better, but he wanted Sam to know that he wasn't alone. They would all be here waiting for him when he got out of surgery.

"I'll be waiting right here for ya, Sam," Danny let him know with a firm nod, promising to be there.

As Sam smiled in response to Danny, Maria slipped between them, leaning over to gaze down at her son with a warm smile.

"My brave boy. You make me so proud to be your Mama. I love you," she told him sincerely, needing him to know that. She wasn't saying goodbye, but she wanted him to have the words with him. She placed her hand over Sam's, her thumb stroking his soft knuckles.

Danny rested his hand over both of theirs, holding them close as they crowded together. He hadn't felt so whole in his life, and it killed him that he had to let Sam go soon. However, he wanted Sam to get better. There was so much promise for the future, and Danny wanted Sam to see it all. He shot a wink at Sam, trying to liven his spirits. It wouldn't do any good for Sam to go into his surgery as a pessimist. Sam had to believe that this would work and that this would be the last surgery for him.

"Givin' up ain't an option," Danny reminded him as he lifted his eyebrows at Sam. His tone had a joking sound to it, but he was far from playing around. He needed Sam to fight with everything that he had, and Danny knew that was asking a lot. He knew how sick and uncomfortable Sam felt.

Sam merely winked back as his gurney started to be pushed away by the medical team. He turned his head to let his eyes trail Danny and Maria as he was guided down the brightly lit hallway, white soon overtaking his vision.

Chapter Seventeen

The Final Act

Two Years Later

The Dolby Theater in Hollywood fell silent as Nikki Holmes, a blonde actress in her thirties who had won the Best Actress award last year, stood by a sleek podium, her silver dress shimmering as much as the golden décor that accented the stage that she stood on. A sea of seats with notable faces and known talents flowed out in front of her in the dimness of the space, anticipation filling the air. A monstrous golden statue stood behind her as if watching over the ceremony.

"They all delivered captivating, resonating, and provocative performances. The nominations for Best Actor are ... Diego Rivera, *The Boat* ... Pierre Duvalier, *City of Light* ..." Nikki's bubbly voice echoed throughout the theater. As she called the actor's names, photos of them as their characters appeared on a big screen behind her, soon followed by a live shot of them sitting out in the crowd.

"... Danny Vitello, *The Homecoming*," Nikki Holmes announced, and a photo of Danny from the movie, similar to his audition scene with Kendra popped up on the screen behind her. A few seconds later, a close up shot of him in the audience sitting calmly appeared on the screen, a black suit adorning his body. Applause trailed her words before the theater fell silent again, anxious to hear the results of the Best Actor award.

Nikki Holmes held up an envelope in front of her, nearly bouncing on the spot as she leaned forward to speak into the microphone.

"And the Best Actor goes to ..." she trailed off as she began ripping open the envelope, nearly tearing it into shreds so that she could read the card inside.

"Yes! Danny Vitello! *The Homecoming!*" she cheered excitedly before clapping.

The crowd followed suit, erupting with applause and cheers as the television cameras swiveled to capture all of the reactions. The people sitting behind Danny went wild, leaning forward to pat him on the back and clap him on the shoulder out of congratulations.

Danny didn't even move for a few moments; his head bowed as he took in the moment that was raining down on him. Two years ago, he had never imagined himself in this situation. He hadn't known where he would end up, but he was glad to be here, to be recognized for all of the work that he had put into the movie. It had helped keep him together in more ways than one. With a smile, he gradually stood up and headed toward the stage, his eyes resting on the golden award waiting for him.

Back at Cedars-Sinai in the nurses' station, Nurse Sally, surrounded by a dozen other nurses who were just as pumped, stared up at a small television monitor that was airing the awards show. Upon the announcement of Danny's win, they broke out into joyful cheers, bouncing up and down and throwing their arms around each other in celebration at the news. Nurse Sally pumped her fist in approval, a proud look adorning her face.

Danny made his way down the aisle toward the stage, his heart hammering in his chest as people applauded him from either side. For so long, he had been used to negative attention or just flat out being turned down. Now, it was all different. Everything had changed, and the thought of how far he had come threatened to bring tears to his eyes.

Kendra Kastle moved away from her seat to greet Danny in the aisle, her arms winding around him to draw him into an embrace, pressing him flush against the blue gown that she wore.

Danny hugged her back, flashing her a grateful smile before continuing on to the stage in front of him. He headed up the steps and met up with Nikki in the middle of it, his hands reaching out to carefully take the award from her hands.

Nikki beamed at Danny as she leaned forward to peck him on the cheek, the crowd cheering in the background.

"So happy for you, Danny! We've all been pulling for you," Nikki congratulated him warmly as she stepped back away from the podium, letting him have the spotlight for his acceptance speech.

Danny smiled at her before moving to the podium, clutching the award to his chest as he gazed out at the crowd once it started to settle. He really hadn't expected to win, so he didn't have an exact speech prepared. Even if he did have every word planned out, he wasn't even sure if he could say them because his throat steadily swelled, disbelief and pride overwhelming him.

"Two years ago, I never thought I'd be here. I don't mean here at this ceremony … but here at all," Danny started his speech, hearing the crowd immediately go quiet after he spoke. He knew that he was venturing into a heavy and dark topic, but he wanted to be honest with the people watching him. People thought that they knew him, but they really didn't. They didn't know what he had gone through over the past few years and even before that when he was away in Iraq at war. They had no clue how it affected him, how it had sent him spiraling.

"A lot of guys never came home from the war, like my brother, Elvis ..." Danny trailed off, his jaw clenching as he tilted his head to look upward. He couldn't look into anyone's eyes right now, couldn't bear to see their sympathy for him. He already knew how awful and sad the situation was, and he didn't need to be reminded that his brother was no longer with him when he should've been.

"... some came back physically wounded, and some with invisible wounds ... for me and others, the war keeps playing in our heads ..." Danny continued before swallowing hard, his eyes beginning to burn. Even now, his past held his mind hostage at times, threatening to shuttle him back into his painful past. He was scarred, and he had accepted that there was no way to cure all of the damage that had been done to him as a result of being in the war.

Danny lifted his hand to draw it across his brow, clearing the beads of sweat that had started to accumulate on his heated skin. It was hard talking about all of this with mostly strangers, but that part of his story deserved to be told and heard. Even if he didn't want it to be, it was a part of who he was, and he wanted people to know the real him. He wasn't that destructive, reckless guy that people used to see him as.

"It took me awhile to take the first step, which was getting help. Glad I did. I encourage all of my brothers and sisters out there to talk to someone. There's people who really care ..." he announced, hoping that they would take him up on his suggestion. Without the help that he had gotten, he knew that things would've been far worse. He knew that his life would be in far more jeopardy, and he couldn't risk that now after everything that had happened.

194

"My battle with PTSD doesn't end tonight. I know that I'll be fighting it tomorrow. too …" Danny said, knowing that there would always be a fight when it came to his own mind. He would always have to be mindful, to watch for the signs that he was threatening to slip back. It was a burden, but he was getting it more and more under control. That was what mattered.

His eyes trailed down to the golden trophy in his hands, a proud ache echoing through his chest. He reached into his pocket to grab a small piece of paper with a list scribbled down on it. He glanced over the page before lowering it from his eyes, deciding against his original plan. Nothing ever went according to plan anyway.

"There are many people that I should thank, but I want to tell you about an amazing little boy, Sam, who lifted me out of a … a really dark place. Sam was very ill, but he never stopped fighting. He fought every day," Danny spoke, his voice the only sound throughout the entire theater.

"Sam was in and out of the hospital for many years for surgeries, chemo …" Danny nearly felt his throat threaten to close up again, forcing him to swallow hard before drawing in a deep breath to steady himself. Sam had struggled so much for so long, and it broke Danny's heart to have to think about that and especially to have to say it.

"When we first met, he told me he was a fan of mine … and then I became a fan of his. He taught me that each day is a gift … that giving up …" Danny had to breathe out the last part, becoming nearly too choked up to speak, but he had to keep going. These words were important, and people needed to hear them because there wasn't enough hope in the world.

"… ain't an option," he managed to say, his eyes blinking rapidly. He breathed in heavily, his grip tightening on the trophy as his hands threatened to tremble. He didn't want to fall apart on stage in front of all of those people, but it felt like he was pulling on his own seams at this point.

"Our time here is short. For some of us, every day, every hour, is a battle. When you find someone who loves you, who believes in you, let 'em know how special they are. Hold onto them … as long as you can," Danny spoke, his voice faltering at times as the strength of it became sapped. He gazed out at the audience, noticing that there wasn't a dry eye out there. Each member of the audience was choked up to some degree. Eventually, his eyes landed on someone out in the thick of the crowd.

"For my beautiful wife, Maria …"

Maria felt eyes draw to her as she stood in the fifth row, a beautiful gown adorning her body and tears filled her eyes. She smiled at Danny, a look of pride on her face.

Soon, the audience's attention shifted elsewhere out of surprise, trailing someone making their way to the stage.

Danny watched with a smile, the tension leaving his shoulders.

"… and my son, Sam," he announced.

Sam, who was taller with a full head of dark hair, bounded up the stairs without any lack of energy, his body now healthier, stronger, and full of color. He threw himself into Danny's arms without hesitation, a warm smile gracing his lips.

Applause and cheers boomed throughout the theater immediately, everyone moving to their feet to cheer.

Danny placed a hand on the back of Sam's head, holding him tightly as the noise of the crowd faded into his background. The fame … the money … none of it mattered at the end of the day. The only thing that really mattered to him was his family, and he held onto them with the promise of never letting them go.

⁓ THE END

Made in the USA
Columbia, SC
04 February 2024

31354843R00114